**Nervously Matt searched
the back of the church one more
time. Again, no sign of Amy.**

Growing tired of smiling at those guests
seated directly behind him, he had no choice
but to turn his attention toward the front of
the church. As he watched his uncle Chad
place Susy's hand in Dave's, he swallowed
hard. He wanted what they had. And in a
selfish moment, he couldn't help but cry out
to God, When will it be my time?

It wasn't that he didn't wish Susy and Dave
all the happiness in the world. He just wanted
a little marital bliss to drift his way....

Books by Crystal Stovall

Love Inspired

With All Josie's Heart #126
A Groom Worth Waiting For #155

CRYSTAL STOVALL

dreamed of writing inspirational romances from the moment she discovered Grace Livingston Hill's novels as a teenager. These books changed her life in a profound way, starting her on a quest to blend faith and romance in her personal life, as well as launching her writing career. She's a graduate of Oral Roberts University and a recipient of the Romance Writers of America's Golden Heart Award.

Crystal lives in Tulsa with her husband, Jim, who is president of the Emmy Award-winning Narrative Television Network. Though she's lived in Oklahoma for nearly twenty years, she's still an easterner at heart. Her frequent visits to her upstate New York hometown—especially a certain boulder on the edge of Cayuga Lake—provide her with the inspiration and perspective that she finds essential to her writing.

A Groom Worth Waiting For
Crystal Stovall

Love Inspired®

Published by Steeple Hill Books™

STEEPLE HILL BOOKS

Steeple
Hill™

ISBN 0-373-87162-7

A GROOM WORTH WAITING FOR

Visit us at www.steeplehill.com

Printed in U.S.A.

...Be strong and courageous.
Do not be terrified; do not be discouraged, for the
Lord your God will be with you wherever you go.
—*Joshua* 1:9

To my sister, Amy—
May your life always be blessed
with an abundance of love and happiness

And to Lila Junk,
who continues to be an angel in my life

Chapter One

This was not at all the way Amy Jenkins had imagined her new life. In her daydreams, she'd pictured a cozy apartment with a fireplace and a courtyard view, a satisfying job that challenged her yet left her fulfilled at the end of the day and a new church family that made her feel like she'd finally come home.

Instead, on this dreary May morning she was lost, tired and hungry. But those problems could all be easily remedied. At the next convenience store she passed, she'd buy a bag of peanuts and ask for directions. And if she spent her money wisely, she had more than enough saved to cover meals and a motel room until the end of the month.

But what couldn't be fixed was the lost feeling in her soul. What should she do next? Where should she go? The questions spun in her head as she drove down the Kentucky highway.

Gripping the steering wheel as if it were a life preserver, Amy prayed the next gust of wind wouldn't blow her into the deep ditch that separated the highway from miles of horse pasture. Between the hard rain and patchy fog, it took all of her concentration to keep the midsize car between the white road lines.

Only two weeks earlier, Amy had closed her eyes, twirled herself around as if she were playing pin the tail on the donkey and pointed to a city on the huge map of the United States she'd hung on the living room wall. For several minutes, she'd stood in front of the map, too scared to open her eyes. She'd promised herself she would move to whatever city her finger landed on. It didn't matter if she pointed to Detroit, Wichita or Chicago, she was relocating. There was no other choice. Still, keeping her fingers crossed behind her back, she'd hoped at least for a warm, sunny climate, such as San Diego or Orlando advertised.

What mattered most, though, was that she put miles between herself and her Ohio hometown. And most important, miles between her and her ex-fiancé, Garry. She opened her eyes and smiled. *Lexington, Kentucky.* It sounded like the kind of city where a girl with a broken heart could make a fresh start.

However, within only a few hours, Amy's carefully made plans had dissolved like sugar in water.

Leaning forward on the car seat, she wiped excess moisture from the windshield with her sleeve in an attempt to improve visibility. Then she almost passed a convenience store and strip shopping center before she spotted them. Hitting the brakes as hard as she dared, she slowed down enough to make the right turn safely. Because most of the parking lot was roped off for construction, Amy was forced to park in front of the dry cleaners, which was three businesses to the right. Turning off the ignition, Amy let out a huge sigh and then rested her forehead against the top of the steering wheel. Between the weather and her worries, she was stressed to the limit.

Oh, God, she prayed. *What should I do now? Was I wrong to come to Lexington? Is this a sign You want me to go back to Ohio?*

She didn't wait for an answer, because there was no way she was going back to Ohio. At least, not for a very long time.

The rain eased, and Amy dashed for the front door. A loud buzzer sounded as she entered the store, and the middle-aged clerk behind the checkout counter instantly looked up and said hello. An easy-to-read name badge identified him as Hank.

Amy returned his friendliness with a smile and then shook her arms and shoulders as if she were part feline. Rubbing her upper arms with her palms, she attempted to warm herself. While the hooded sweatshirt and fleece pants were comfortable, they weren't quite warm enough for the cold front that had moved through the city the night before. However, her warmer clothes were in storage, and since the chilly weather wasn't expected to last more than a day or two, it hadn't seemed worth the trouble to retrieve her coat.

Realizing she was the only customer in the store,

Amy said, "It looks like the construction has hurt your business."

"Not really," Hank said. "You just missed the morning rush. We've been here for years. Our customers won't let a little inconvenience scare them away."

"That's great," Amy said. "Where do you stack today's paper?"

"In the aisle to your right." Hank watched as she selected a newspaper, turning away only to answer the telephone.

With the paper tucked under her arm, Amy headed for the back of the store, intending to grab a soda until she spotted a cappuccino machine. Even though she wasn't crazy about convenience store coffee, the thought of drinking something hot cheered her. At the same time she set an empty to-go cup in the machine and pushed the proper sequence of buttons, the front door opened and the loud buzzer sounded again. As Hank had with her, he looked up from his paperwork and greeted the stranger.

"Hello," he called, watching the man in the tailored suit just as he'd observed Amy.

Making his way down the aisle with hurried strides, the confident-eyed man asked, "How fresh is the coffee?"

"The pot just finished brewing and the bagels were delivered first thing this morning," Hank assured him.

It wasn't until the tall stranger turned the corner that Amy realized he was headed straight for her.

"I don't know how you can drink that stuff," he

said, pointing to the coffee, milk and sugar mixture that streamed into her cup. Picking up a glass coffee-pot, he poured himself a cup of regular coffee and selected a sesame seed bagel.

Amy shrugged, thinking that if the man really wanted to strike up a conversation, he could have opened with something a little more friendly. Removing the steaming coffee cup from the machine, she took a sip and smiled at the stranger as if this were the best cappuccino she'd ever tasted.

But it wasn't, and Amy turned away to hide her grimace just as the door buzzer sounded again and two men dressed in gray work uniforms entered. As the clerk called out his greeting, Amy felt a measure of safety knowing Hank was alert and observant. It only took one more sip to convince her she couldn't finish the drink. Like the handsome stranger had said, it was awful. But it was warm. Pressing the paper cup against the side of her neck, she enjoyed the warm print it left on her skin. For the first time all morning, she felt a moment of relief.

Everything will work out, she told herself. Some-how, she would put her life back together. She'd find another job and an even better apartment. But as for men, it would be a long time, if ever, before she trusted her heart to anyone.

Moving the cup across her forehead and down her cheek, Amy reveled in the heat. Sensing the stranger beside her move, she stepped to the left to avoid a collision. Before she could look up, she felt the man's hand cover her mouth at the same instant he yanked the coffee cup from her hand and tossed it to the floor.

From the front of the store, she heard someone call, "I'll check the rest of the store to make sure we're alone."

Held tightly against the stranger's chest, she didn't have time to think as he pulled her around the pyramid of motor oil cans, just missing a perfectly balanced stack of cheese crackers.

She struggled, making little impact against the man's grip. With his hand clamped across her mouth, he pinned her head against his hard chest. When she tried to scream, she found she could barely open her mouth enough to breathe, let alone to bite him.

The last thing she glimpsed as he backed through the vertical blinds that hung in the narrow opening between the retail space and the storeroom was her newspaper and cappuccino splattered across the beige tile floor and a man at the front of the store pointing a gun at the clerk who'd been so nice to her.

Though the man in the suit continued to hold her firmly, Amy didn't stop struggling. If only she could break free. If only she could make a run for the door.

Oh, God, she prayed, *help me. Protect me. Please, Lord, let me get out of this alive.*

The storeroom was dim and cool, and the stranger who'd preferred his coffee black and fresh steered her to a back corner.

"You can trust me," he whispered.

Amy didn't move a muscle. Not even to breathe.

Trust him? She didn't trust any man, let alone

someone who'd just abducted her. And how did she know he wasn't part of the plan? That he wasn't a foil for the man holding the gun?

In an instant, Amy recalled every talk show and news story she'd ever seen that had given tips on how to survive a threatening attack. *Listen to your instinct. Fear is your built-in radar detector,* she remembered a safety expert saying.

Amy believed that the inner radar detector was really God's voice. However, for the last month she'd been so mad at God she'd given Him the silent treatment. She wasn't too sure she could depend on His help. And besides, her heart was beating so loudly she didn't know if she could hear His voice even if He shouted at her.

"You have to trust me. It's our only chance," the man whispered as he quietly guided them along the back wall. He moved with a certainty that suggested he knew where he was and where he was headed.

Amy had no choice but to move with him. Together, they stumbled a few steps, and when her feet didn't move in unison with his, he lifted her and pulled her into a tiny closet.

No sooner had they reached the hiding place than the light in the storeroom flashed on and they heard the squeak of rubber shoes on the tile floor. Doors were flung open, but in his haste the man overlooked the narrow closet door. Then the light flashed off and they heard the squeaky-soled man yell, "No one in the back."

Though darkness engulfed them, Amy's eyes adjusted quickly to the lack of light. The square closet was cramped and filled with mops, brooms and pungent cleaning products. Because the stranger had backed in first, Amy faced the door, which was open just a crack. The only light, a narrow beam, came from a high, tiny barred window on a far wall.

"If you promise not to scream, I'll remove my hand."

Amy swallowed hard. Blood raced through her veins and perspiration dripped from her brows. Could she trust this man?

Something deep inside her said yes.

Besides, what choice did she have?

The more time elapsed, the more she became convinced the stranger who held her tightly was as much a victim as she was. Nodding slowly, Amy silently promised she wouldn't yell for help.

Hesitantly, he removed his hand, letting it hover near her lips until he was certain he could trust her. As she studied his hand in the thin ribbon of light, she sensed he was an honorable man. While his hand was large, there was a softness and dexterity in the curve of his fingers that revealed a sensitive nature. And though his nails were manicured and clean, calluses on his fingertips suggested he enjoyed working with his hands. However, the image didn't mesh with the business suit, silk tie and expensive cologne.

For the first time, Amy wished she'd paid more attention to the man who still held her firmly with one arm. If her life depended on describing him, all she'd be able to say was he was of average height and weight, with blue eyes, light brown hair and a commanding voice. And he smelled so heavenly that the woodsy scent temporarily distracted her from the pending danger, causing her to think of verdant meadows and fast-running clear streams.

Just as she felt she could trust the man, he startled her by reaching into his suit pocket. Immediately, Amy froze as a hard object pushed against her side. She'd been wrong to trust him even a little. When she realized he was punching a number into a cellular telephone, she bit down on her lip to curtail a loud gasp.

The man spoke in a voice just above a whisper. "I'm at the Quick Stop convenience store. There's a robbery in progress. I'm hiding in the storeroom with a woman who was also in the store. I don't know what's going down out there. I saw two men, and at least one has a gun. There've been noises which indicate a struggle, but we can't see anything from back here. They don't know we're in the store, but I can't be certain."

Amy listened with amazement at the information the man relayed. She'd been so wrapped up in her own troubles that she hadn't paid much attention to anyone else in the store. And while she sensed the ordeal might be far from over, at least with the police on the way she felt she had a chance of leaving the closet alive.

Instantly, a prayer formed in her mind. *Dear God, let the police get here before it's too late for us and the clerk.* Even though she couldn't see the stranger's face, she knew without a doubt that he sent the same prayer heavenward.

Two angry voices splintered the silence, followed by the sound of shattering glass. Amy jumped at the noise, and the man embraced her with both arms. This time, though, she didn't fight his closeness. She took the comfort and strength he offered, and leaned into his protective circle.

"We're going to be okay," he whispered. Though his voice sounded confident, she knew he was just as scared as she was. Finding his hand, she squeezed it, and he squeezed back.

The voices shouted at each other again, and Amy pressed against the man. Turning her head as if she couldn't bear to see what was happening in the next room, she rested her ear against his chest. Finding comfort in the fast but even rhythm of his heart, Amy soon realized that her own cadence matched his.

Outside, car doors slammed. Then the store telephone rang. Someone answered on the third ring. Amy could only assume the police had arrived, and with their presence she prayed this terror would soon be over.

The man turned his ear toward the door, and Amy could tell he, too, was listening for clues as to what was happening on the other side of the wall. However, it was impossible to make any sense of the random noises. One thing was becoming very clear, though; something had gone wrong. Neither of the two voices belonged to the friendly clerk. The robbers were fighting with each other, and who knew what that could mean.

Amy did the only thing she knew to do. She prayed harder and faster.

And as if the man sensed the urgency of her messages to God, he clasped her hands as if to say he wanted to join in her prayers. Because she didn't dare whisper any more than was necessary, Amy moved her lips as she prayed silently, and from behind she felt the man's warm breath on her neck as he, too, prayed.

When they got out of the closet, she would owe this man her life. And somehow, she'd find a way to repay him.

Matthew Wynn held his breath as glass crashed to the tile floor, and each time the woman jumped, he tightened his grip on her arms. Though he was playing the role of protector, he'd never been more scared in his life.

For what seemed like forever, the shattering noise came in waves, as if a madman were swooping down the aisles with widespread arms, knocking dozens of jars to the floor. Matt couldn't begin to guess what was really going on in the convenience store or why the police hadn't been able to apprehend the robbers. Over and over, he searched his mind for a way to bring this situation to an end, but came up with no safe solution. For the moment, it seemed enough that he protect the woman in his arms.

Matt didn't need to see her eyes to know she feared

for her life. He felt her terror in the tremble of her hand, in the way she pressed against his chest as if she couldn't get close enough and in the way she'd turned her head as if she couldn't bear to face the truth. And yet, despite her fear, she'd reached out to comfort him. She'd let him know with the squeeze of her hand and a reassuring rub on his forearm that she believed if they worked together they'd leave the storeroom alive.

Finally, the crashing glass stopped, and both Matt and the woman exhaled at the same instant. Though Matt loosened his embrace, he noticed she didn't move. In the silent lull, a storeroom clock ticked off the seconds. Though it felt like they'd already been held hostage for hours, Matt guessed the actual time was closer to a half hour. Feeling his legs cramp, he shifted his weight, and he wasn't surprised when the woman's movements shadowed his own.

Dear Lord, he silently prayed, *show me what to do. Help me protect this woman, and please, Lord, keep Hank safe.*

Though Matt didn't know the clerk well, he thought the world of Hank's father, Howard, who owned a local chain of convenience stores. Howard had given Matt his first job, and he'd worked in this very store until after college graduation. Back then, he'd had no clue that his knowledge of the storeroom layout might one day save his life. The closet they were hiding in had been added as an afterthought, and instead of having a real door, a makeshift one had been fashioned out of a leftover piece of wood paneling. Because the door blended into the paneled walls, the robber hadn't noticed it when he'd searched the storeroom.

When the silence continued, it became more unnerving than the crashing glass and angry shouts. What could be happening out there? Should he leave the closet and peek through the doorway? It was their only means of escape, as the delivery entrance was generally locked at all times, and the only window was barely big enough for a dog to crawl through. Plus, it had bars. But even a peek seemed like too much of a risk. If it had been just his own life, he would have taken the chance. But he had to consider the woman, too.

As the silence drew out and the woman's heartbeat raced his, his thoughts turned toward her. He'd never seen her before, but that wasn't unusual in a city the size of Lexington. She'd caught his attention the instant he'd seen her by the cappuccino machine. Not just because she was attractive, but because there was a sad turmoil in her eyes that made her seem fragile and lost. He'd wanted to say something profound, but what could you say to a stranger? Instead, he'd barked out something silly about her cappuccino. Then she'd amused him by smiling as she'd sipped the sugary drink. He knew she didn't like it but drank it just to spite him. And he felt that same spunky spirit now as they patiently prayed for their freedom.

Suddenly there were a hundred questions he wanted to ask her. Like where did she live and what did she do for a living? How did she happen to be in this convenience store this morning? Did she believe in God? Did she love to ride horses across grassy meadows? Did she like corn dogs and chocolate ice cream cones? It seemed silly in this tense moment to wonder these things. Yet it was better than focusing on what could happen if things went wrong.

Without thinking, he brushed his hand across the top of her head, memorizing the silky feel of the fragrant strands. He swallowed hard, desiring to rub his hand down her cheek and neck and across her arms. As if, in the simple touch, he could know this woman. But he knew that was impossible. He sensed her complexity. This was a woman of spirit and passion, yet graced with enough common sense to trust him in this dangerous moment.

The shouting started again, but Matt couldn't understand what was being said. Instinctively, he tightened his embrace as the woman pressed against him. Leaning his head close to hers, he whispered, "It's going to be okay. It's going to be over soon."

In response, the woman placed her hand over his, and in the long, desperate squeeze communicated her faith in him and God. And as her message pulsed through his body, Matt felt something more profound and more deep than he'd ever experienced before. He felt as if he knew this woman in ways he'd never understood another woman. He felt as if she could see through the darkness to his vulnerabilities, to his longings, to his failures, as well as his hopes and dreams for the future. It was crazy, but he felt closer to her and more connected to her than he'd ever felt to anyone in his life.

He shook his head in an attempt to break the bond between them, to prove it didn't exist, to prove it was merely a figment of his imagination. But the magic permeated the storeroom just as the scent of warm cinnamon bread lingered in the kitchen long after the last bite had been swallowed.

For just a moment, Matt didn't want the standoff to end. He wanted to go on holding this woman forever.

The woman's body stiffened, propelling Matt back to the danger at hand. The noises had changed. The front door buzzer sounded, and new voices filled the room. He thought he heard the click of handcuffs but couldn't be certain.

When she tilted her head toward him as if to ask if it would be safe to go out, he answered by pulling her closer. He wouldn't risk her life by venturing out too soon.

Finally, a gruff man, who identified himself as a police officer, shouted from the storeroom doorway that it was okay to come out. Matt and Amy sucked in their breaths, leery of leaving their safe nest.

"Dear Lord," Matt prayed, "thank You for keeping us safe."

Amy finished, "And thank You for sending a guardian angel my way. I don't know what I would have done if I'd had to face this ordeal alone."

"We made it through together," Matt said, then squeezed her hand.

The police officer charged into the storeroom and opened the closet door. Both Matt and Amy exhaled in unison.

"There's a man and woman in here," the officer called to his partner. Immediately, two paramedics rushed in carrying medical equipment. Even still, Amy remained in the stranger's protective embrace until a paramedic pulled her free.

Chills suddenly descended upon her, and in that instant, she felt more alone than she ever had before. She looked at the nameless stranger's blue eyes and thought she saw her anxiety mirrored on his face. She wanted to reach out her hand, to draw them together again, but a flurry of uniformed men blocked her silent plea.

"Are you hurt?" the paramedic asked, glancing from Amy to Matt.

"I'm fine," Matt said. "Please, help her."

"I'm okay," Amy insisted. For the first time, in full light, she looked into her protector's eyes and was overwhelmed with gratitude. "If it hadn't been for this man's courage and quick thinking, I hate to think what might have happened."

Amy stammered over the last words, and the tears that she'd been too frightened to cry began a slow descent down her cheeks.

With a gentle flick, Matt wiped the tears away, then pulled her close. With his arms around her tightly, he felt as if order had once again been returned to his world.

As if it were the most natural thing to do, he kissed

the top of her head, and he would have been happy to never let go. She felt so right in his arms. She felt like the woman he'd been searching for. The woman who would bring an end to his lonely life and fill his dreams once again with hope.

Reluctantly, he let go of her so the paramedic could check her physical condition. Whether it was by chance or God's design, this woman had suddenly come into his life, and he didn't want to let her walk away. He wanted a chance to get to know her, to discover if she was everything he believed her to be.

The officer in charge waited until the paramedic finished examining both of them, then said, "I'm going to need your statements."

Amy and Matt both nodded.

"And Hank?" Matt asked, anxious to know if the clerk had survived.

"He's going to be okay. He had a heart attack during the robbery, but he's on the way to the hospital," the officer explained.

Matt's jaw dropped. "Oh, my gosh. I had no idea. So what happened out there?"

"At this point, we can't be certain, but Hank's heart attack probably saved his life. The best I can figure, he had the attack about the same time they pointed a gun at him."

"But why didn't they just shoot him and run?"

"We may never know the answer to that." The officer shook his head, raising his brows over perplexed eyes. "These two men are wanted in other states for similar robberies. And they're not stupid.

Being convicted of robbery is a far cry from murder or manslaughter. Regardless, they'll both be going away for a long time."

Matt still didn't understand. "You'd think when things got botched, they would have taken the money and run."

"It's called greed. Hank was in so much distress he couldn't open the safe. One of the guys had seen a commercial that claimed aspirin could save a heart attack victim, so he forced Hank to take aspirin. However, by the time Hank responded you'd already made your call and the store was surrounded."

"And so they panicked and argued about how they were going to get out of this mess."

"You could say that. The one guy went berserk and in a rage destroyed everything in the store. Listen, if you'll have a seat, I'll be back in a few minutes to take your statement." The officer went into the retail area.

Matt met Amy's gaze and for the first time realized he didn't even know her name.

"I'm Matt Wynn," he said, extending his hand.

"I'm Amy Jenkins," she answered, grasping the hand that had been her lifeline for the last hour. "I don't know how I'll ever repay you. I owe you so much. You saved my life."

Matt shook his head. "I didn't do that much."

"You saw what was happening and you reacted quickly. If those men had seen us, there's no telling what would have happened to us."

The thought of anything happening to Amy distressed Matt. Though he'd only known this woman an hour, he couldn't bear the thought of harm befalling her angelic face.

"I want to try to make this up to you. You have to let me find a way to repay your courage and kindness." Amy's eyes pleaded for him to accept her offer.

Once the crazy idea popped into his head, Matt pushed it aside. However, he wasn't prepared to let Amy walk out of his life, either.

"There is something you can do for me," Matt finally said.

"What?" Amy asked, her eyes brimming with gratitude.

"Assuming you live here in Lexington, you can be my date…to three family weddings this summer."

"Your date to a wedding?" Amy repeated as if it were the most outrageous idea she'd ever heard.

Matt looked away, anticipating her rejection. And if she did, he wouldn't embarrass himself further by trying to persuade her.

"Yeah." He tried to explain as if it were no big deal. "I've got three cousins getting married this summer, and there are few things worse than going to a family wedding without a date."

Amy looked at him for a second, emotions he couldn't read flickering in her wide brown eyes. He was certain she was going to say no.

"You did save my life." She swallowed hard, as if this was the hardest thing she'd ever said in her life. "I suppose it is the least I can do."

"Then you'll be my date?"

Though Amy smiled as she nodded, Matt saw the terror in her eyes. The prospect of being his date at the weddings frightened her more than the morning's ordeal had.

He instantly wished he could take back his invitation, but it was settled. Amy Jenkins, for better or worse, would be his date to three family weddings.

Chapter Two

If she'd thought she'd had a choice, Amy would have said no. Definitely not. Going anywhere near a wedding ceremony was out of the question. The mere thought of bridal gowns, lace veils and cascading bouquets gave her the heebie-jeebies.

When he'd given her an out, she should have said she was from out of town, just passing through Lexington. It wouldn't have been a lie. At this point, she didn't know if she was going or staying.

But the man had saved her life, and in the fervor of the moment, she'd promised to do anything to repay his bravery. Why couldn't he have asked her to do something simple, such as cooking his meals or washing his car for the next year? On top of everything else that had happened, a date to a wedding was one more headache she didn't need.

Determined to back out of her promise before it became more complicated, Amy decided to tell Matt while she still had the nerve. After all they'd just been through, he couldn't have been thinking clearly, either. He probably regretted acting on impulse as much as she did.

Touching Matt on the arm, she tried to get his attention, but failed. His body blocked the doorway between the storeroom and the retail area, preventing her from seeing whatever he stared at. Curious, Amy moved toward the door, only to have Matt stop her.

"Let's stay in here a little longer," he said.

While Amy appreciated his protectiveness, she wasn't about to let him shield her from the truth. Though she couldn't push past him, she did lean forward enough to see around him. She gasped. The convenience store looked like a tornado had ripped through it. Smashed bottles of soda, ketchup and pickles, as well as every other kind of food that came in a glass jar, speckled the beige tile floor. The white shelves and refrigerated units sat empty and exposed, their contents heaped in careless piles.

"Wow," Amy said, realizing that the situation had been more volatile and dangerous than she'd imagined.

With her hand covering her mouth, she thanked God for sending Matt to save her. If Matt hadn't been at her side… She couldn't finish the thought. And she couldn't tell him she wouldn't be his date. She owed this man so much more than a few hours at a family wedding. This was a small price to pay for saving her life.

Having seen enough, Amy took a few steps backward. Matt quickly retrieved two chairs from the end of the room that served as an office area for the convenience store manager.

"Can I get you a glass of water or a soda?" he asked.

Amy shook her head, amazed he could remember to be so polite at a time like this. Then she noticed his nervous hands. As if it were beyond his means to control, he repeatedly clenched and unclenched the hands that had held her tightly. She understood then that his desire to attend to her needs was merely a way of covering his own distress.

"I guess we're both still in shock," Amy said.

Matt nodded. "Everything is just now sinking in."

They lapsed into silence, neither able to put into words the intense feelings that surged through their hearts and minds.

Feeling too vulnerable to look at Matt, Amy focused on her trembling hands. Even pressed against her abdomen, they shook. Then his hands covered hers, bringing with them a warmth that made her feel safe.

Amy wasn't certain how long they sat with their hands entwined. She just knew she wasn't ready to let go of this stranger. She wanted to know more about this man who'd unselfishly helped her. Was he from Lexington? What did he do for a living? Had he ever suffered from a broken heart?

When the police officer cleared his throat, Amy glanced quickly at Matt, then suddenly felt foolish for the way she clung to him. Gently pushing his hands away, she concentrated on recreating the sequence of events in her mind.

"Let's start from the beginning," the officer suggested.

"I got here first, and I was the only one in the store besides the clerk. I picked up a newspaper and then made a cappuccino." Amy's voice quivered until she noticed the amusement in Matt's eyes.

"And for the record," she said, "it was the worst cappuccino I've ever tasted." She ignored the officer's impatient glare. The lighthearted comment relaxed her enough to continue. "The door buzzer sounded again, and that's when Matt walked in."

Matt picked the story up from there. "I said hello to Hank, and then I hurried to the back of the store to get a bagel and a cup of coffee to go. I'd promised to stop by Aunt Lila's, and I was already running late. I said something to Amy about the cappuccino. I remember she had her back to the door when the buzzer sounded. By chance, I happened to look up and see the two men enter, and for some reason, I had this feeling something bad was going to happen. Because we were in the back near a stack of oil cases, they didn't spot us. As soon as the man with the beard pulled the gun on Hank, I grabbed Amy and shoved her into the closet. One of the men made a quick check of the storeroom, but because the closet door is made from the same paneling as the walls, he overlooked the closet. From that point on, we didn't see anything. We heard plenty of unidentifiable noises and shouting. But we didn't move."

"Is there anything you'd like to add to this story?"

"I wish I could have done more to help Hank. But I was afraid that if I entered the store I'd only put him in more danger, and I didn't want to leave Amy."

Amy shook her head. While Matt had supplied all the facts, he'd left the heart of the story untold. There was the way he'd held her tightly. The way his moist breath had crawled down her neck. The way his heartbeat had filled the tiny, square closet and had turned the cramped space into a safe refuge. And even more important were the roller-coaster emotions that still traveled on invisible tracks between them.

Turning toward Amy, the officer said, "I need an address and telephone number where I can reach you."

Amy bit her lip as she was painfully reminded that she was temporarily without a home or a job. Inhaling deeply, she said, "I've just arrived in Lexington…this morning…and I don't have a permanent address yet. But I'm planning to stay at the hotel near the airport until I can find a place. I'm headed over there to check in as soon as we're finished," she promised.

"Do you have a work number?"

"I thought I had a job and an apartment, but they both fell through this morning. But that's another story," she said, hoping to conceal the embarrassing state of her personal life.

The concerned expression on Matt's face bothered her. It was almost as if she could see another hare-brained idea percolating in his deep blue eyes. She may have needed his help during the robbery, but only she could put her life back together. No one could help her find her place in the world again or rebuild her relationship with God.

Turning toward Matt, the officer wrote down an address as well as home and work telephone numbers that meant little to Amy. But in another week or so— if she stayed—she'd know her way around Lexington.

Thinking they were free to go, Amy walked into the convenience store, only to come face to face with a crowd of media reporters. With microphones thrust in front of their mouths and bright lights glaring in their eyes, Matt and Amy once again recounted their story. And when Matt got to the part of the story where they were huddled in the storeroom closet, he paused to look at Amy for just a second. It was a moment the reporters missed but a moment Amy would always remember. She had shared something extraordinary with this man that she would never forget. In those closet moments, they'd lived in an unreal world where their fears and hopes had meshed into one.

But this was the real world, Amy told herself. Matt Wynn was a stranger and a man. And she'd learned the hard way that if you trusted a man he would eventually break your heart.

When the media prolonged the interview, Matt gripped Amy's arms and with a move that caught both the media and Amy off guard, he guided her through the store, out the door and into his car.

After locking the doors, Matt quickly left the parking lot and headed down the highway.

"Now, why did you do that?" Amy demanded.

"I was doing us both a favor," Matt said. "The media wanted to make a lot more out of this story than there was."

"You're talking about the way they focused on us being in the closet together for over an hour."

"Exactly. They'll make a mountain out of a mole-hill." Matt concentrated on the road, which was still wet, though at least the fog had lifted and the rain had stopped.

"And nothing happened in the closet," Amy said, wanting to be very clear on this point.

"No, nothing happened. Well, we can't exactly say that. We shared a very unique experience, but that was all."

Amy looked out the window. He'd said precisely what she'd wanted to hear, and yet his declaration left her disappointed.

Turning toward him, she asked, "Then why am I in the car with you, and where are you taking me?"

"To Aunt Lila's," he said as if his response should make perfect sense.

"To Aunt Lila's?" she echoed.

"Like I told the police officer, I was on my way to see Aunt Lila before we were detained at the convenience store. The local stations always cut into programming when there's a crime or emergency in progress, and if Aunt Lila didn't have her television on, I'm sure someone in the family did and has called her. She won't be satisfied until she sees both of us in person and she can judge for herself that we're both fine.''

Amy started to object, but closed her mouth. What choice did she have? She couldn't exactly jump out of the car. She'd go see his aunt Lila and then she'd take a cab back to the convenience store to pick up her car and her meager possessions, which were stored in the trunk.

Glancing at Matt, she sensed an urgency behind his serious countenance. He was up to something, and she had an uneasy feeling his plans involved her.

Matt turned onto the long, winding drive, which was edged by a white wooden fence. Though he didn't look at Amy, he felt a huge measure of satisfaction at her awe-inspired gasp. Even though he'd driven this quarter-mile drive thousands of times, he never took its beauty nor its history for granted.

When the main house and stables came into view, Matt couldn't resist stealing a glance at Amy. With widened eyes, she didn't miss a single detail of the two-story white antebellum home that had been in his family for five generations. Turning slightly, she shifted her gaze to Aunt Lila's formal garden, then to the white barns and corrals, all of which were framed by low rolling hills and a lush meadow on the north and east. He purposely kept his back toward the west so the sprawling housing development wouldn't intrude on the picture-perfect horse farm.

''It's beautiful,'' Amy said. Leaving the car, she

completed a slow three-hundred-sixty-degree turn. "Do you live here?"

Matt shook his head. "It belongs to my aunt. However, I oversee the upkeep for her, so I spend a lot of time here. Plus, she boards my horses."

"You have horses?" Amy asked.

Matt nodded. "Do you ride?"

"Oh, no," Amy said, shaking her head for emphasis. "But I once had dreams of owning a horse until my father explained that a collie puppy would make me just as happy."

"Well, if you're going to live in Lexington, you'll have to learn to ride."

Amy shook her head again. "Maybe later. I'm going to be pretty busy for the next few weeks."

Matt looked toward the grassy meadow while he silently debated whether it was wise to even consider his plan. After all, what did he really know about this woman? One quick glance at her intent eyes squelched his doubts. He'd held this woman in his arms for an hour, and while he might not know much about her life, he knew enough about her heart and spirit to believe he wasn't making a mistake. And if Aunt Lila felt she could trust the woman, too, then that would confirm his instincts.

"You told the officer you were between jobs," he said.

"Yeah," she answered, obviously unwilling to volunteer any more information than necessary.

"What kind of work are you looking for?"

Amy looked at the ground, then let her gaze roam

the green vista. In that moment, he wanted to view the Wynn land through her eyes. Did she see the same beauty he did, or did she just see another wide-open space ripe for development?

When Amy finally met his gaze, he sensed a hesitation that grew from embarrassment. "Actually, I'm looking to change fields and I'm not certain what I'm going to do. I'm thinking of going back to school. If I do, I'll need something that will pay the rent, yet be flexible enough to accommodate my class schedule."

Matt read more into the response than he believed Amy wanted him to. Guessing her age to be mid-twenties, he further assumed she'd never really decided what she wanted to do with her life. It was a feeling he understood too well. He had worked several dead-end jobs after college before settling down in a career as an accountant. But it was his hobbies—the horses and the Wynn family land—that truly satisfied his heart. He chose to work as an accountant in order to make a living for the family he one day hoped to support, but he was most content and fulfilled when he was riding or caring for his horses or walking on the land where his great-grandfather and grandfather had walked before him.

"So, you'd be open to a variety of positions," Matt clarified. When Amy hesitated before answering, he knew it wouldn't be easy to get her to go along with his idea. But then maybe he was pushing too hard to keep her in his life. Still, he was convinced Amy and his aunt Lila were a perfect match. While his plan served his desire to keep Amy in his life, it also greatly benefited his aunt. And Aunt Lila's health and well-being were major concerns of his, as well as the rest of the Wynn family.

"At this point, I can't be picky," Amy finally admitted.

"Well, maybe I can help," Matt said, deciding to leave it at that until Amy and Aunt Lila had had a chance to meet.

Silently, he sent a prayer heavenward. *Dear Lord, if it's Your will for Amy to stay here, let Aunt Lila and Amy both see how much they need each other.* It was out of his hands for now. It was in the care of someone who saw the bigger picture.

The front door of the stately house flew open, and Aunt Lila stepped onto the wide veranda. A month ago, she would have run across the yard with both arms flung wide, eager to hug him and feel for herself that he was okay. But recent surgery had slowed the sixty-year-old woman down, and for the first time Matt was worried about the aunt he adored. Then he saw her bright, youthful smile, and fifteen years melted from her countenance.

Taking off at a jog, Matt rushed toward her. She hugged him tightly, then sandwiching his chin between her agile hands, she looked him over.

"I've been watching the live coverage on TV. You had me worried," she said, a glimmer of tears in her eyes. Though she'd never had children of her own, it hadn't stopped her from spoiling Matt as if he were hers. "You don't know how glad I am to see you."

"To tell the truth, I was a little worried, too,"

Peering around Matt, Aunt Lila said, "And you must be Amy Jenkins."

The older woman extended her hand, and Amy gracefully accepted the warm welcome.

"I'm pleased to meet you. I owe your nephew my life."

"I suspect you had to depend on each other in order to survive," Aunt Lila said matter-of-factly. "And after such an ordeal, you must be starving. I set out an early lunch. You can tell me everything while we eat." Pointing a finger at Matt, she said, "Don't leave out a single detail."

"Aunt Lila," Matt protested. "You shouldn't have. You know the doctor released you from the hospital on the promise you'd take it easy."

Looking beyond Matt, Aunt Lila spoke to Amy. "You understand, dear. There's nothing like puttering in the kitchen to soothe the nerves. Besides, my sister, Louise, brought a roast and deviled eggs yesterday. I just set them on the counter. You'll have to help yourselves."

Amy smiled with understanding, and Matt felt a glimmer of hope.

The lush pastures, the magnificent home and Aunt Lila's feisty spirit were too much for Amy to take in at once. Several times she'd lost track of the conversation and hadn't realized Aunt Lila had spoken to her as her gaze roamed the spacious kitchen, admiring the unique collection of antiques or enjoying the view through the large window. At first, she worried that she'd offended the woman with her wandering mind, but she soon realized Aunt Lila was pleased to find Amy entranced with the home she dearly loved.

To her surprise, she answered Aunt Lila's questions when she'd been reluctant to share personal information with Matt. For some reason she couldn't fully identify, Aunt Lila put her at ease. She felt comfortable in this house, and after the unsettling morning, she wasn't in a hurry to leave the older woman's nest.

"They said on the news you'd just moved here." Aunt Lila pushed her food around her plate, then nibbled on an egg.

"I grew up in a small Ohio town," Amy volunteered. "There wasn't much opportunity there, and when I decided to leave, Lexington seemed like a great place to make a fresh start."

Aunt Lila nodded as if she understood completely what Amy meant, though that was impossible. From a corner chair, Matt sipped a cup of coffee while he quietly observed the exchange between the two women. Amy hadn't given him a second thought until the curious look in his eyes turned smug. She had the oddest feeling that this moment was progressing exactly as he'd choreographed. And that bothered Amy.

"How long ago did you move here?" Aunt Lila asked.

"Today was my first official day."

"Oh, my," she exclaimed. "What a fine welcome you've received!"

"This morning was certainly more exciting than I'd hoped for," Amy admitted.

Aunt Lila rose slowly, refilled the coffee mugs, then set a plate of sugar cookies on the table. "They're Matt's favorite. I know as long as I keep them stocked he'll keep hanging around."

Matt smiled, as if he'd heard this comment before. "Now, Aunt Lila, don't be giving away my secrets so soon."

"Don't be certain this young woman hasn't already seen clear through you," Aunt Lila quipped.

"What's there to see?" Matt joked. "I'm an open book."

Amy looked from Matt to his aunt, suddenly feeling like the outsider. She'd been right, Matt was up to something. Impatiently, she stood, having had enough of the conversation. "If there's something to be said, I wish someone would come out and say it. Otherwise, I've got to be going. While I appreciate your hospitality, I've got important matters to attend to." Like finding a place to live and a decent job.

Matt opened his mouth, but didn't say anything.

"Well," Aunt Lila prodded. "Are you going to ask her or do I have to?"

"I'm not sure what you mean," Matt said.

Aunt Lila rolled her eyes.

When Matt didn't respond quickly enough to please Aunt Lila, she charged ahead. "It's fairly simple, actually. I'm only a few days home from the hospital, and my family is worried that I'm overdoing it.

They've tried to convince me to hire help, but until now I've refused."

Amy nodded, beginning to understand the situation. "And your nephew knows I'm out of work, not to mention that I'd like to repay him for his courage."

Matt leaned forward in his chair. "Well, it just seemed to me that you both—"

"What do you think, Amy?" Aunt Lila interrupted.

"I don't know what to say. You don't really know me." *And I don't know you at all*, she thought. Though the offer seemed to be the answer to her immediate problems, was it prudent to move into the home of a virtual stranger?

"We'll need to exchange references, of course," Aunt Lila said, taking charge. "We could give it a try. See if it works, and if it doesn't, what harm has been done?"

Amy bit her lip. "I don't want to sound ungrateful, but I need time to think this over."

"I'd like to sleep on it, too. Let's trade references now. That way we can both make an intelligent decision by tomorrow evening."

Amy glanced at Matt, and by the amusement in his eyes knew the situation was as much out of his control as it was hers.

Amy was relieved when Matt didn't talk on the drive back to the convenience store. He saw her safely to her car, then waited until she'd driven off. As she watched him through her rearview mirror, the oddest feeling overwhelmed her. She felt like she was leaving her best friend behind, and yet twenty-four hours ago she hadn't even known him.

Forcing thoughts of Matt from her mind, she focused on the task at hand—securing a room for the night. When the hotel near the airport turned out to be more expensive than she felt she could afford, she passed it up. An hour later, she settled into a budget motel near the interstate. Despite the thin walls and veneer furniture, it was new and clean, and the woman who'd checked her in had assured Amy several times it was safe. Though the clerk didn't come right out and say so, Amy had the distinct impression she'd recognized Amy from the news.

Only one day in town, and she'd already made a splash. This was hardly the fresh start she'd planned. Yet, there was much to be thankful for, and she wouldn't forget that. She thanked God for safely seeing her through the day.

"And Lord, I know we haven't been on the best of terms lately, but I'd really like to change that. I'm just not sure how. I know You haven't abandoned me. You proved that today. Don't give up on me. I'm really trying to find my way back to You."

She sat for a few minutes in silence, and her thoughts turned to Teresa, her close friend from high school. They'd had a big falling out during their senior year, over a boy, of course, and hadn't talked for months. And when they did try to rebuild their friendship, the first few meetings had been awkward and uncomfortable. Yet, she'd always known Teresa would have been there for her in a pinch if she'd really needed a friend. That was sort of the way she felt about God right now. When He'd sent Matt to protect her, He'd proved He hadn't abandoned her. But the lines of communication remained strained, and it would take time and effort to get back to the level of faith and trust she'd treasured before her ex-fiancé had destroyed her innocence.

As for things between her and God, she had a lot of hope. However, it would be a long time, if ever, before she'd trust her heart to a man.

Those thoughts led her back to Matt and Aunt Lila's proposal. But before she could even entertain their offer, she needed to decide whether or not she would stay in Lexington. She had no ties here. Maybe losing the job and apartment this morning that she'd secured two weeks ago on her initial visit, along with the robbery, were signs from God that she didn't belong here.

But if she didn't stay in Lexington, where would she go? Who was to say bad luck wouldn't follow her wherever she went? A quick check of her wallet convinced her Lexington was the practical choice. She only had a limited amount of funds, and she didn't want to spend her nest egg looking for another city and moving her belongings. She'd already seen how quickly the expenses added up. If she was going to make it, she needed to be settled with a job yesterday.

Maybe she was supposed to go home.

But she didn't want to go back to Ohio.

And it wasn't just because of the humiliation she

felt every time she bumped into Garry in public, which in her small hometown was often. No, much more was at stake than her pride.

Between Garry's betrayal and the robbery, she felt vulnerable and unsure of her own capabilities, and she needed to prove that she could take care of herself. That she could make it on her own. If she went back to Ohio, she'd never have the opportunity to prove this. Her parents, though well-meaning and loving, would shelter and protect her.

In the lonely motel room, she admitted to herself and God what she wouldn't admit to anyone else. She was scared. But deep in her heart she knew this was a turning point in her life, and what she decided today would affect her forever. She could go back to the past she knew, or she could move forward to an uncertain but promising future.

Lost in silent prayer, she felt the peace that had eluded her for months. She would stay in Lexington.

But as she considered the pros and cons of Aunt Lila's offer, that answer was not so clear.

Matt recognized the blue car as soon as it came into view, traveling slowly up the meandering driveway. He was certain Amy had returned in order to politely turn down his aunt's offer. And why shouldn't she? Taking care of Aunt Lila while she recuperated from surgery wasn't exactly an exciting career move.

Latching the corral gate, Matt jogged toward the main house, leaving the horses and stables behind. In

shape from the many hours he spent working out-
doors, he wasn't a bit winded by the time he reached
Amy. Approaching her as she shut the car door, he
realized how glad he was to see her.

"Hello," he called.

Though Amy shielded her eyes from the late afternoon sun, she wasn't able to conceal her surprise, and
perhaps even her disappointment.

"I thought you'd be at work." She turned away
briefly. "I didn't mean that like it sounded. It's good
to see you," she added with false brightness.

Though he couldn't be certain, he sensed she felt
the same mixed emotions he did. It was crazy that a
woman he'd just met could capture his interest so
quickly, and he couldn't help but wonder if she were
the one. No, he had to let those thoughts go. He didn't
believe in love at first sight. Love took time to grow
and mature, and as lonely as he was and ready to
settle down, he wasn't going to do anything foolish.
Still, what harm would it do to take the time to get
to know this woman? To find out if something special
could grow between them.

Matt swallowed hard, his Adam's apple sticking in
his throat as he looked into Amy's bewildered eyes
and instantly knew that if she left today he'd never
see her again. Oddly, that made him feel sad. Yet, if
that was God's plan, then it was for the best.

"This is such a lovely farm," she said.

As her gaze wandered, he realized she was stalling.
That perhaps her mind wasn't made up.

"Are there any questions I can answer for you?" he asked.

Amy pursed her lips as she gave the matter serious thought. "We didn't discuss specific terms yesterday. I really need to know more before I can make a decision."

"Then you're interested?"

Amy nodded. "Your family has a sterling reputation. I'd be remiss not to consider working for your aunt."

"You checked us out?" Knowing she was treating this offer seriously pleased him.

"I called the references, plus I stopped at the library to do some research on the Internet. Your family seems well established and respected. I understand they've played an important role in Lexington's past."

"That's true," Matt said with pride. And he hoped to do his part by preserving the family property, where it all began.

"If you stay in Lexington, you're bound to run into us Wynn cousins. We're a pretty active bunch."

"And about this job?" Amy asked, as if she had dismissed any qualms she might have felt concerning the family.

"Basically, we'd like you to live with Aunt Lila and oversee the house and her needs. Your job would include everything from light housework and fixing meals to making sure she takes her medication on time and to help her with the exercise routine her doctor prescribed. Most importantly, you'll need to make sure she doesn't try to do too much too fast.''

Amy smiled. "And I have a feeling that's harder than it sounds."

Matt grinned, too. "Trust me, I've already tried and failed. She's a stubborn woman with a heart of gold. And when she gets an idea in her head, there's no stopping her."

"Gee, I wonder who takes after her."

Matt shook his head, enjoying the light banter.

"Does this mean you'll take the job?" Looking directly at Amy, he held his breath as he waited for her answer.

Biting her lip, Amy still couldn't make up her mind. For some reason she couldn't explain, she wanted to say yes. But before she did, she wanted to make sure she was saying yes for the right reason. That she was doing what was best for her and not what was easy.

After having paced the motel room floor for most of the night without reaching a decision, she'd hoped once she reached the Wynn farm the answer would be obvious. And maybe it would have been if Matt hadn't been here. Though she wanted to show her appreciation for the unselfish way he'd protected her during the robbery, she didn't want to take the position out of obligation.

When Aunt Lila called, both Amy and Matt looked up. "Where are your manners, Matt? Show the lady to the house." When neither moved, Aunt Lila waved them to come in.

"You heard my aunt," Matt said.

"Yeah," Amy said. As they walked toward the house, she found her answer. This home and this woman had a spirit that drew her. It was as if God had provided a safe haven where she could heal her broken heart.

She would help Aunt Lila get back on her feet, and in return, she'd use this opportunity to take stock of her life and make plans for the future. After all, this was only a temporary arrangement.

Chapter Three

Aunt Lila clasped her hands and smiled. "I'm glad to hear my prayers haven't gone to waste. I have a hunch this arrangement is going to work out for both of us."

Amy reached out to shake the older woman's hand and was immediately pulled into a loose embrace. Though surprised by Lila's enthusiasm, she appreciated the warm welcome. Still, for someone who'd refused to hire help, insisting she could make it on her own, Lila had quickly changed her mind. But that was a family matter, and Amy decided right then and there not to get caught up in the Wynn family business. She'd been hired to assist Aunt Lila and nothing more.

"I hope you're right," Amy agreed. "Finding a job and a place to live in one day is better than winning a sweepstakes. And I'm going to do everything I can to make your recovery as comfortable and easy as possible.''

"Oh, I have no doubt this arrangement is going to work out." Though Lila appeared tired, a strange sparkle lit her eyes as if she knew a special secret. "And now, if you don't mind, I'm going to lie down."

"What can I do to help? Perhaps I could bring you a cup of hot tea? Or maybe you'd like me to run some water for a bath?" Amy asked, feeling like there was no time better than the present to get started.

"Oh, no," Aunt Lila insisted. "I'm going to rest, and then after dinner we'll discuss how you can best help me."

"At least let me prepare dinner," Amy offered.

Lila nodded with approval, then turning toward Matt said, "In the meantime, I'd like you to help Amy move her things into the south guest room and then take her on a tour of the property."

Being a fast learner, Amy already knew better than to argue with Lila. However, she didn't intend to spend the rest of the afternoon with Matt, and she was certain he'd feel the same way.

Amy and Matt both nodded as if in agreement, then waited until Lila had left the room before honestly facing one another.

"What was that about?" Amy asked.

"I'm not sure what you mean." Matt shrugged, as if to say he truly was clueless.

"That look in your aunt's eye."

"Oh, that," Matt said, shaking his head. "There's

no telling what she's dreaming up. Trust me, you'll get used to seeing that sparkle. Aunt Lila's always got a plan.''

"Like what kind of plan?"

"Let's see. She's always redesigning the gardens or remodeling the house. And if she's not doing something to the house or barns, then she's helping raise money for a favorite charity or she's working on a church committee. Her specialty is weddings, and lucky for her, her nieces and nephews have kept her plenty busy recently.''

Amy noticed Matt's wistful eyes, but because she wanted to avoid any talk of weddings she let the look pass without comment.

"I gather Aunt Lila's a very active woman."

Matt grinned. ''That would be an understatement.''

"Sounds like I may be the one who has a hard time keeping up.'' From the brief time she'd spent with Lila, she knew she was going to enjoy working for this woman. Lila possessed a zest for life that was contagious, and Amy already felt a sliver of the woman's optimism taking root in her own heart.

"She'll keep you busy," Matt agreed. "But I really think you'll be a great team. Otherwise I wouldn't have suggested this arrangement in the first place.''

"And I want to thank you for introducing me to your aunt. Without this job and home, I might not have been able to stay in Lexington.''

"Well, you did get off to a rough start."

When Matt looked at her, she shivered, suddenly feeling the same electric connection she'd felt between them during the hour she'd spent in his arms in the storeroom closet. And then the moment passed, leaving her face-to-face with a kind stranger. Disturbed by her fluctuating thoughts, Amy determined it was time to end the visit.

"I owe you a lot. And I promise I'll take good care of your aunt."

"I know you will." Then, clasping his hands together as he looked toward the door, he said, "Let's get your things moved in and take that tour."

"Really, I don't expect you to waste your afternoon. I don't have much in the car, and I'm certainly capable of wandering around the property on my own. In fact, I'd enjoy it. So, please, don't feel obligated. I know Aunt Lila only wanted to make sure I felt welcomed, and you must have more important things to do." Even before she finished the long speech, Amy knew she wasn't getting through to the man. Her words bounced off his grin as if they were made of rubber.

Matt shook his head. "Your job's going to be a whole lot easier if you learn from the start not to ignore Aunt Lila's orders. I'll never hear the end of it if I desert you now. Besides, it won't take that long to see the property."

Amy bit her lip in an attempt to stop the frown in progress. The same sparkle she'd seen in Aunt Lila's eyes now simmered in Matt's. While she didn't want to start off on the wrong foot with her new employer, she wasn't all that convinced Lila would really be upset if she took a rain check on the tour. If she hadn't known better, she'd think Matt had his own reasons for wanting to stick around. Sighing, she realized he probably wanted to get to know her better. After all, he'd brought a stranger into his aunt's home. He was probably having second thoughts and needed some assurance that he'd made a wise choice.

"Okay." Amy gave in. "But just a quick tour."

Then after dinner, she'd call her parents and assure them she was okay. In fact she was better than okay. As she met Matt's gaze, she couldn't help but feel her fresh start was going to be everything and more than she'd dreamed it would be.

As Matt carried the last suitcase into the grand foyer and up the wide, twisting stairway, he tried to see this house through Amy's eyes. Was she intimidated by the high ceilings, Palladian windows, tapestry fabrics and miles of the finest polished mahogany? Or, despite the grandeur, did she feel the warmth, love and coziness that lingered from years gone by?

Matt set the suitcase next to a lopsided pile of boxes and bags. Amazingly, everything on the floor had been stuffed into the trunk of her mid-size car. And yet, considering she had just moved to Lexington, it wasn't much at all.

"Is there anything else I can help you move?" he asked, thinking she might have left a rented moving trailer parked at the motel.

Amy shook her head, and as if she read the curiosity in his eyes said, "When I came to town two weeks ago on my scouting trip, I put the majority of my things in storage.''

''And that same trip you found a place to work and live?''

''Yeah, I thought I'd found the perfect job. I was going to be the leasing agent at a small apartment complex. Free rent was one of the perks. Not to mention the flexible hours and that I could have afforded to at least take a part-time load at the university this fall. But that all fell through this morning. There was a mix-up. Apparently, the man who hired me didn't know the owner had already hired someone else.''

''Wasn't there anything you could do?'' Matt asked with great concern.

''Not really. The person they hired had already moved into the apartment. You know what they say about possession being nine-tenths of the law. The man who hired me claimed he tried to telephone me when he realized what happened, but I'd already left Ohio.'' Amy rubbed her eyes and pushed her hand through her thick brown hair. ''Even if I had a strong case, I don't have the means nor the inclination to take them to court.''

Tilting his head and offering a wise smile, Matt said, ''Things have a funny way of working out.''

Amy merely rolled her eyes and walked to the window. As she tentatively pushed aside the sheer drape, creating a small opening to peek through, Matt studied her profile for clues as to what she might be thinking and feeling. But her stoic countenance gave little away. Swallowing hard, he found himself at a sudden loss for words, wondering if he were crazy for bringing this woman into his aunt's house. What on earth had possessed him? She was a stranger, and in this awkward, silent moment, he felt it profusely.

But she was a beautiful stranger.

While her eyes followed a restless black thoroughbred across a distant pasture, he watched her. He loved the way her silky dark brown hair graced the tops of her shoulders. And anyone with such fair skin certainly couldn't spend endless hours in the summer sun. Instead, he imagined her sitting on his aunt's veranda in the old rocking chair, sipping cold lemonade and nibbling on sugar cookies. With perspiration glistening on her slender neck, she would gently fan herself.

Matt turned away and took a deep breath. This was his loneliness talking. He'd always thought he'd be married by now. Instead, he had been best man to a string of cousins, and by the end of the summer he'd be the only unmarried Wynn cousin. And he didn't even have a prospect in sight. That was, until he'd held Amy in his arms. Even though he'd been terrified during the life-threatening ordeal, he'd found a certain comfort in holding her close. It was as if his subconscious had taunted, *This is what it would feel like to hold a woman you could love for a lifetime.*

Shaking his head, Matt physically tried to suppress the ridiculous thoughts. While it was true he felt an unexplainable bond with this woman, it wasn't love. Love didn't happen in a flash or even in an hour. Real love, like the kind his parents and grandparents shared, took time to grow and mature. Glancing at Amy, he promised himself he wouldn't blow their newfound connection out of proportion. They had survived a dangerous moment together. It was only natural he should feel drawn to her.

Feeling more confident, Matt moved to Amy's side. As they stared out the window in silence, he resisted the urge to casually drape his arm across her shoulders. When he turned his head, he found her studying him with curious eyes. He smiled, and when he did, her composure cracked, and he saw the distrust, confusion and sadness she tried to hide. In that moment, Matt could only wonder why God had brought this woman into his life.

"How about that tour?" he asked, suddenly anxious to stretch his legs and inhale the fragrant Kentucky air.

They hadn't walked very far when Matt realized Amy skillfully redirected the conversation each time it headed her way. While Matt wasn't trying to be nosy or rude, he did wonder what had brought her to Lexington and why such a beautiful woman would be content to work for his aunt for the summer.

There were so many things he wanted to ask her. But as he'd learned from his horses, patience was a virtue. Given enough time, she would tell him everything he needed to know.

As they left the formal rose garden and started to follow the trail that wound around a small hill behind the estate, Amy stopped to take one last look at the large two-story white farmhouse, the expansive lawn and the series of white barns.

"It's postcard perfect," she said, admiration showing in her eyes.

Matt inhaled deeply, pleased by her enthusiasm. Next to family and friends, there was nothing he loved more than this one hundred acres.

"No matter what season it is, the view from here is spectacular." Matt shielded his eyes with his hand as he let his gaze shift from the horses in the pasture below to the main stable with the towering clock tower and chimes that could be heard across the property, and then finally to the huge shade trees surrounding the house. The wooden swings he and his cousins had played on as children still hung from the sturdy branches. Someday, his children would swing beneath those oaks.

He felt Amy's gaze upon him like a warm shadow. "This farm means a lot to you," she said. He couldn't be certain, but he thought he heard envy in her voice. And that made sense. His roots went deep, while she had yet to replant. It was as if she carried her heart and soul in a small container, transporting them from city to city, looking for the right place to dig in. Respecting her privacy, he resisted the urge to ask her what she was searching for.

"The land's been in my family for five generations. It's where I find my strength. It's where I've learned who I am and what I'm going to be." He hoped he didn't sound lofty or arrogant. That wasn't his nature.

But it was hard to put into words how this place defined his life.

"This is where you meet God," Amy wisely said.

"I never thought of it like that," Matt said. But she was right. And suddenly a host of memories flooded him. He saw himself as a child walking this trail, wedged between his father and grandfather, listening as they talked of faith and hope and family loyalty. Things he was only beginning to truly understand.

"My grandfather always said, 'You walk life out one day at a time.' I guess I took him literally."

Amy bit her tongue as if she were trying to gather her thoughts. "What if you didn't have this land?"

"I can't imagine that," he said. He'd already told Aunt Lila that when she was ready to sell, he would purchase what still remained of the once thousand-acre horse farm. While everyone in the extended family loved the farm, no one else wanted the responsibility.

"No, that's not what I mean. What if you didn't have a place where you could come to God. Would you still be able to find Him?"

Matt started to answer quickly with a yes, but stopped himself when he realized her question must stem from her own search for God. This hill was where he came when he was troubled, when he needed to sort things out, when he wanted to draw closer to God. He glanced toward the top of the tree-covered hill and realized he couldn't separate his relationship with God from this property. They were entwined like the ivy vines that covered the south side of the house.

"It's easiest for me to find God here," Matt finally said. "But God is in my heart. He goes wherever I go. Maybe it would take some time to relearn how to talk to Him if I didn't have this outdoor sanctuary, but I would find a way to reach Him."

Amy nodded, as if she were storing away each word for later retrieval. "I admire your confidence."

In that split second, she caused him to reexamine his faith. Because he had been raised in a Christian family and surrounded by a loving extended family, believing in the power of God had come naturally. He witnessed it constantly when he walked barefoot through dewy bluegrass, when he inhaled the sweet fragrance of a cherry blossom or when he felt the rush of the spring wind against his face and neck as he rode his favorite mare across the meadow. And now he had to ask if he'd taken this heritage for granted. Maybe if he'd come from a different background, as this woman obviously had, he might not have found God so easily as a child.

Matt pursed his lips, then spoke with a grin. "Why don't you give this hilltop a try and see what you find."

Amy smiled back. "You'd share your special place with me?"

Enjoying the playful moment, Matt admitted, "It's kind of like sneaking a girl into the boys-only tree house, but I think there's room for us both on this hilltop. In fact, I'll race you to the top."

Before he finished issuing the challenge, Matt began the sprint up the steep but wide dirt trail. Glancing over his shoulder, he saw Amy at his heels. Then within seconds, she reached his side, her breath even and strong. "You didn't tell me you jogged."

She smiled as she rushed past him to the top.

Even before she reached the top, Amy heard Matt's footsteps slow. She took the few minutes of privacy he offered without question.

Shutting her eyes, she tilted her head back, letting the warm sunshine and breeze cleanse her. When she opened her eyes, the view from the small plateau was breathtaking. She could see for miles in all directions. Underneath the puffy blue sky, highways and housing developments crisscrossed horse pastures and meadows as the old and the new merged into one landscape. In the distance, she recognized the downtown Lexington skyline.

Though Amy couldn't see Matt, she knew when he approached by the scent of his cologne. It was the same woodsy essence he'd worn when they'd been trapped in the closet, and she would forever associate it with the safety of his arms. So when his arm brushed against her shoulder as he stood behind her and pointed to the horizon, she didn't flinch.

"See that row of trees?" he asked.

Amy nodded.

"That's the original property boundary. If you follow it, you'll be able to trace the original tract of land."

With his free hand on Amy's shoulder, they slowly rotated together. While she looked everywhere he directed, nodding at just the right moments as he pointed out the meandering stream, the rolling pastures and his prize thoroughbreds, her focus remained on him.

He spoke directly into her ear, so low and soft that his words resonated throughout her body. His breath caressed her neck like a gentle mist, while the spring breeze blew his scent as if it were made of silk, twisting around her body until she couldn't move.

When he pointed out the housing development that now occupied nearly a third of the old homestead, his frustration and despair vibrated through her body.

"The developer actually did a great job of blending the homes into the landscape. He kept as many of the native trees as he could, he designed around the natural contour of the land and he even dug a pond and installed a natural stone fountain as the architectural centerpiece of the development."

Even from the plateau, Amy could see the water spray high into the air. And she thought if she listened hard enough, she might hear the beads splash against the surface.

However, the admiration in his voice surprised her. "I thought you'd be bitter. I mean, I barely know you, and yet it's obvious how much this family home means to you."

"Yeah, I wish my grandfather and uncle could have held on to the entire tract of land, but I understand the economic reasons behind their need to sell off parcels. I probably would have made the same decision they did.''

"But it still upsets you," she said. She hadn't imagined his frustration.

He paused while his gaze perused row after row of houses. "I think what bothers me most is that this is a change that can't be undone. The clock can't be turned back on this development. The natural beauty, the innocence of the land is gone forever.''

Amy held her breath as he talked, thinking for a minute that he spoke about her. But that was impossible. He didn't know how Garry had betrayed her days before their wedding. He didn't know how Garry had humiliated and deceived her. In one careless moment, Garry had stripped her of her self-confidence and her trust in God and left her with a broken spirit. And like the land below, she would never be the same trusting, easy spirit she'd once been.

The wind picked up, swirling dust around Amy's feet. She inhaled deeply, and for the first time since she'd left Ohio she felt a tingle of hope. Hope that here in Kentucky she could rebuild her life. And hope that on this hilltop she'd find her way back to God again.

"You're awful quiet," Matt said.

Amy pressed her lips into a half smile. She knew what Matt was really saying. *I've told you a little about myself, now it's your turn.*

"I was just thinking about how different this farm is from the small town where I grew up." She proceeded with caution, not certain how much she would tell Matt.

"In Ohio," he said, without looking at her.

Maybe it was because he gave her the space she needed, or maybe it was because she needed to release pent-up emotions, but either way she decided to tell him enough to satisfy his curiosity.

"Just north of Cincinnati," she said.

"And you have family or friends in the Lexington area?" he asked.

"No, in fact, I'd never been here until two weeks ago when I came to see if I could find an apartment and a job."

"And when you did, or at least when you thought you had, you loaded up and moved here."

"What?" she said, thinking she'd mistakenly read a mix of astonishment and admiration in his blue eyes.

"That takes a lot of guts to pack up and move to a new city."

"Sometimes life doesn't give you much of a choice." As soon as she'd spoken, she felt like she'd been tricked, as if he'd somehow forced her to admit the truth.

When he didn't immediately probe, but instead let the silence stretch between them like a taut rubber band, she felt compelled to ease the tension. "I'm not running away." She wanted to be clear on that. She could have stayed in Ohio.

"You don't strike me as the type who would run away."

She looked at him for a minute, making sure his eyes reflected the confidence in her that he claimed to have. "There's a difference between running away and running to something." Until this moment, she really hadn't seen it that way herself. "I knew that if I'd stayed, my anger and resentment would have destroyed me. And I couldn't let that happen."

"So how did you end up in Lexington?"

Amy smiled as if she were about to share great wisdom. "I tacked a map to the wall and played pin the tail on the city. And ta-da!"

Matt reached out and smoothed a strand of hair behind Amy's ear. "I don't care how you came to Lexington, I'm just glad you're here."

"You are?"

Instantly, Matt's smile became wider as if to hide his true feelings. "Sure, you're the perfect companion for Aunt Lila. You don't know how worried the whole family was about finding help she'd accept."

"Right," Amy said. "And this is the perfect arrangement for me, too."

Turning slightly away from him, she closed her eyes and listened to the distant cries of restless birds, the thrashing of squirrels jumping from tree to tree and a lone plane slicing through the puffy clouds. Even though she felt out of sync with God, she believed with all her heart that He'd brought her to this piece of heaven to heal her broken heart. She didn't care how long it took. She wanted to rid her heart of the anger and resentment and hurt that still lingered.

She wanted to feel whole again. And someday, she hoped she'd be able to love again.

Matt's woodsy scent grew stronger, and she realized they stood back to back. In the quiet moment, she flashed back to the time they'd spent in the closet. It was funny how she felt closest to him when they shared the silence.

Matt cleared his throat. "Um. Just so you can mark your calendar, my cousin Susy is marrying Dave in less than three weeks from today. You'll get to meet most of the family then, as well as my parents. I expect they'll drive down from Louisville for the day."

Amy would have laughed if it hadn't hurt so much. Just when she was feeling a glimmer of hope, he had to go and ruin a perfectly lovely afternoon with the mention of a wedding.

"Oh, my gosh," Amy exclaimed. "I had no idea how late it was getting. I promised Aunt Lila I'd fix dinner."

Before Matt could respond, Amy started down the hill. All the way to the house, she waited for his woodsy scent to catch up with her, but it never did.

Chapter Four

Lost in dreamland, Amy restlessly rolled across the large four-poster bed. Pulling the worn but colorful quilt over her head, she attempted to block out the irritating tap, tap, tap. When the knocking continued, she muttered, "Okay, okay." Using both arms to raise her upper body, she started to get up, but when her rubbery muscles failed, she collapsed against the soft mattress and dozed off.

The bedroom door opened, its hinges creaking with the weight of age. Startled, Amy jerked up, suddenly aware the knocking was real and not part of some weird dream. Anchoring tousled hair behind her ears, she tried to clear the sleep-induced fog from her mind.

"Oh, dear," Aunt Lila said. "I didn't mean to wake you. I was certain I'd heard you stir earlier, and, well, I thought you'd like to start the day with a cup of hot tea."

Still covered with the patchwork quilt, Amy rested

her chin on her knees. Glancing at the clock, she saw it was nearly nine o'clock. She silently groaned. This was no way to start her new job.

"I'm so sorry I overslept, Aunt Lila," she said, as she bounced from the bed and grabbed the robe she'd left on the chair. She'd been so tired the night before she hadn't even unpacked. The few belongings she'd brought from Ohio still lay in the center of the room in one unsightly heap. Another strike against her.

Lila handed her the cup of tea and pointed to the chair. Meekly, Amy slunk into the channel-back seat and sipped the warm liquid.

Sitting in a matching tapestry chair near the window, Lila watched her closely and smiled when Amy said, "This is wonderful."

"I always start the day with green tea. It's good for you."

"But this is *really* good."

Lila winked. "It's my own special blend."

Still feeling self-conscious, Amy said, "Tomorrow morning, I'll make the tea, as well as your breakfast."

"If you insist," Lila said, seemingly unperturbed. "However, today I want you to take it easy. You've been through a lot—"

"But you're the one who should be taking it easy."

"Nonsense," Lila said, waving her hand. "I managed before you came. Besides, there's nothing pressing. We can both take the day off."

Amy couldn't help but admire the elder woman's spunk and independence. And she couldn't help but hope a bit of Lila's confidence would rub off on her before the summer ended.

Lila continued, "I may have had the surgery, but you've been through a pretty rough time yourself." Pausing, Lila glanced out the window as if to reconsider whether she should speak her mind. "I know this is none of my business, but hiding in the closet had to have been traumatic, and if you need to talk about it, I'd be willing to listen. Or if you'd like, I could introduce you to my niece who's a counselor. I'm sure she could help you. Or should I call Matt?"

"Oh, no." Amy shook her head. "I wouldn't want to trouble him. He's done so much already."

"I know he'd want to help."

"Really, I'm fine." Moved by the woman's kindness, Amy's eyes dampened. "I obviously slept well."

Lila smiled as if it were impossible for anyone to not sleep well in her beloved home.

"The whole ordeal has left me a little shaky, but I think I'm okay. Though I may avoid convenience stores for a while." Amy laughed, and Lila grinned with her. And Amy planned to avoid Matt Wynn, too. Just because the handsome stranger had saved her life didn't mean they had to become best friends.

"Despite the danger and uncertainty, Matt made you feel safe and protected," Lila said.

Amy nodded, amazed at the woman's insight. Safe and protected weren't the only things she felt when Matt was near. There was a connection between them unlike any she'd ever experienced before, and it confused her. After the heartbreak her ex-fiancé had caused her, the last thing she wanted was to feel drawn to another man. She would be Matt's date for three weddings, as she'd promised, and she'd stay with Lila through the summer. Certainly by fall, she'd find a job with a future, an apartment she loved and a new church family. But she couldn't say these things to Lila. So out of respect, she said, "I don't even want to think what would have happened if Matt hadn't been at my side."

"And you shouldn't think about it. Not for a second." Lila pointed her index finger with authority.

The two women lapsed into a comfortable silence as they gazed out the window at the rolling hills and sunny sky. In the distance, a band of thoroughbreds grazed across a green pasture.

"I tell you what," Lila said. "Let's take a short walk, and then you can have the rest of the day to unpack your things and get acquainted with the house. My nieces and nephews have brought in more than enough food to last a week."

"I intended to put in a full day," Amy said as she drank the last of the green tea.

"I know, dear. But as you'll soon find out, there really isn't that much to do. Though, if you promise not to breathe a word to my family, I'll admit I'm glad you're here."

Once again, Amy noticed the sparkle in the older woman's eyes and wondered what thought had ignited the gleam. "Your secret's safe with me."

"The doctor said it would take most of the summer

before I got my strength back. And, well, on the chance I might fall, or heaven forbid have some sort of episode, it comforts me to know you won't be far away.''

Amy nodded, and as she looked into the woman's gray eyes, she saw a flicker the rest of the family had missed. Lila was lonely. A woman who was used to being on the go and who genuinely loved being surrounded by friends and family was suffering from her family's recent coddling.

''I'll give you the space you want, yet stay close enough in case you need help. In fact, maybe we should buy cellular telephones.''

''That might not be a bad idea,'' Lila agreed. ''I love this old house, but it's so large you might not hear me if I needed you. If I had a small phone I could carry in my pocket—that'd be perfect.''

''I'll buy us each one this afternoon,'' Amy said. Realizing how difficult it must have been for Lila to admit her need for a companion, Amy changed the subject. ''How about that walk?''

''It sounds grand. I thought we could take a short stroll through the garden.''

Located behind the house, the formal garden stretched deep and wide and was surrounded by a high, thick hedge. Though Lila was slightly winded by the time they reached the entrance, the mere sight of late spring flowers brushed her face with a healthy glow.

Guiding Lila to the nearest bench, Amy suggested they rest for a moment. Leaning on Amy's arm for support, Lila slowly lowered her lean body to the concrete bench.

"I don't know when I've ever seen a more heavenly garden," Amy said. "It must require a lot of work."

"Ah, it does," Lila said. "But it's worth every callus and backache."

From where they sat, beneath a series of arbors laden with climbing roses, Amy had a clear view of the garden. Crisscrossed by winding cobblestone paths, the verdant sanctuary appeared to contain many rooms. Endless rows of irises, begonias, daisies and hollyhocks were complemented by trailing wisteria, lilacs, phlox and a multitude of other beautiful flowers, shrubs and trees Amy couldn't identify. Eventually, all the stone paths led directly to a circular reflecting pool. Rising from the mirrored surface was a three-tiered fountain topped by an angelic figure.

"My great-grandmother started this garden," Aunt Lila volunteered. "I have her diaries. Of course, it wasn't this big or this grand back then. She was young and newly married, and times were rough. All this grew out of a small herb garden. Over there." Lila paused to point at a distant corner of the garden that was tilled and marked like a vegetable garden. "She used the herbs for both cooking and healing. But the real power was in the growing."

Amy nodding, understanding exactly what Lila meant.

"She called it her worry garden."

"A private place where she could let go of her burdens and trust them to God," Amy finished.

Lila smiled. "The garden needs to be tilled again, and this year's herbs planted. I'm not up to the task this summer, so I'd like you to take over for me."

"Me?" Amy said, unable to hide her astonishment. "But I've never gardened before." Though she'd watched her parents putter in a small plot behind their suburban home, she knew virtually nothing when it came to weeding, fertilizing and nurturing tender plants.

"We'll do it together," Lila assured her. "I'll donate my expertise, and you'll lend the labor."

"Okay," Amy said, feeling a bit more confident.

"Trust me, it'll be good for what ails you," Lila said.

Amy glanced at the herb garden then back to Lila and knew few things escaped this wise woman's notice. Once again, Amy felt the flare of hope. It would be good to make something grow, to witness the handiwork of God daily. And maybe, just maybe, between Matt's hilltop and Lila's garden, she could find the peace and the reconnection to God she so desperately sought.

For the next ten minutes, they toured the formal garden, walking slowly, arm in arm. All the while, Lila recounted family history and shared gardening tips. When they reached the entrance and turned toward the house, Matt emerged from the closest barn and waved. Wearing blue jeans, a denim shirt and cowboy boots, he looked every bit the weekend horse enthusiast.

Without hesitation, Lila motioned her nephew to join them. Worried the older woman might be over-tired, Amy strongly suggested they go back to the house, adding Matt could catch up with them there, and by the time he did, Amy would have made her escape.

Much to Amy's dismay, Lila remained put.

"Good morning, ladies," Matt said, as he approached with long strides. After kissing his aunt on the cheek, he greeted Amy by tipping the bill of his baseball cap. Though perspiration and grime streaked his face and neck and dust and hay speckled his wind-blown hair, Amy thought him more handsome than he'd been in his tailored suit. Beyond the change of attire, the real difference simmered in his blue eyes. Matt had obviously spent the last few hours doing what he loved most in the world—working with his horses.

"Lila's been showing me the garden," Amy said. "But I think it's time we head back to the house."

"I'll walk with you," Matt said to Amy's disappointment.

Aunt Lila extended both arms, and as one, the trio moved slowly toward the back veranda. Once there, Lila slipped into a rocking chair, intent on talking to her nephew.

Before Amy could politely excuse herself, Lila asked Matt if he might be free for the next few hours.

"If you need something, I'm your man," Matt cheerfully volunteered.

"Great. I thought you could take Amy on a tour of the city. I want to know that if I send her out on an errand she'll be able to find her way home." Lila glanced from Amy to Matt with a stubborn smile that would be impossible to deny.

"That won't be necessary. I'm a great map reader. Plus, I wanted to pick up the telephones as well as a few other items this afternoon. I'm sure Matt has better ways to spend his Saturday."

"I doubt it," Lila said with certainty. "And while you may be able to read a map, you'll need Matt to fill you in on the history. There's lots of history in these parts, and the Wynns have always been a big part of it."

How could Amy argue with family pride? Still, she gave it one more try. "A drive would take a while. I don't feel comfortable leaving you alone for such a long stretch."

"Nonsense," Lila said. "This is the weekend. There'll be a parade of nieces and nephews through here from now until sundown. Won't there, Matt?"

Matt nodded. "She's right. My cousins always stop by to check on Aunt Lila and to ride."

"Plus, this afternoon, we're going to go over the last details for Susy and Dave's wedding. You know it's only two weeks away."

At the mention of a wedding, Amy suddenly changed her mind. "I can see you're going to be well taken care of. Maybe this would be a good time to let Matt show me around.''

Aunt Lila grinned like a woman with a secret.

Matt was astute enough to realize Amy didn't want to spend the afternoon driving around Lexington. It wasn't until Aunt Lila had mentioned Dave and Susy's wedding that she'd changed her mind, and that surprised him.

He'd assumed the fascination with bridal satin, Edinburgh lace and tiered cakes was genetic. For years, he'd listened to his female cousins and sisters plan their wedding days down to the smallest detail. And though he'd mercilessly teased them, not once had he let on that he, too, had big dreams.

At first he thought Amy's desire to skip the afternoon planning session might be because she felt as if she were intruding. But instinct told him there was a deeper reason. And that intrigued him.

So, despite the fact he'd planned to spend the afternoon working with the horses and most of the evening at his accounting office trying to get a jump-start on the upcoming week, he'd told Aunt Lila he'd be happy to spend the afternoon with Amy.

''I'll give you the abbreviated tour—two hours at the most,'' he promised as they walked toward his sports utility vehicle. ''This way we keep Aunt Lila happy, and you still have time for whatever you had planned to do this afternoon.''

Amy nodded without a speck of enthusiasm. She

pulled dark sunglasses from her tote bag and hid her eyes, as well as any hint of what she truly thought.

"You'll need this," he said, handing her a folded map.

"Thank you, but I already have several maps of Lexington."

"I'm sure you've got a good road map, but this is the official Bluegrass Country Tour Map."

Amy sighed loudly. She crossed her arms and turned her head to look out the passenger window as the vehicle sped down the long driveway and turned onto the highway. It was obvious something troubled her. But instead of letting her indifference about the tour upset him, he felt challenged. If it took all afternoon, he'd make Amy fall in love with Lexington. He'd make her see these gentle hills and endless pastures with the same passion he did. He'd make sure she never wanted to go back to Ohio.

"This'll go a lot faster if you work with me," he suggested.

Amy glanced at her watch as if the afternoon couldn't be over soon enough. Finally, she looked directly at him and offered a small smile. "What would you like me to do?"

"If I'm going to drive, I'll need you to read the map."

"Don't tell me you might get lost?" Her smile widened, and Matt had the distinct impression she'd been able to push whatever worried her to the back corners of her mind.

"I'm not going to get lost. I haven't been lost since

my senior year of high school. And that night, it was on purpose.''

When Amy rolled her eyes and laughed, Matt longed to stare openly at her. Her melodious voice stirred his soul with happiness and joy, and just as it had in the convenience store closet, the desire to know this complex woman overwhelmed him. He wanted to know what made her smile, what made her cry. He wanted to know her dreams as well as her fears.

With a mental shove, Matt pushed these thoughts to the side. Then he silently reprimanded himself for making too much out of the connection he'd felt with this woman during the robbery. Whatever had passed between them wasn't real. With time it would diminish.

''Then if you're not going to get lost, why do we need the map?''

''It's for you to follow along.'' Using one hand, he reached across the seat and helped her open the map. When his fingers accidentally brushed against hers there was no jolt of electricity. Matt bit his lip with satisfaction, pleased to have proof that the attraction between them had already begun to wane. ''There's a route mapped out. Points of interest are marked with a number, and then there's a corresponding paragraph or two of description or history.''

''I see,'' Amy said, showing the first signs of interest. ''And we're here,'' she said, pointing to Harrodsburg Road.

"If we'd gone south on this road, it would have taken us to Shaker Village."

Before Matt could continue, Amy jumped in. "A restored nineteenth-century Shaker community which features twenty-seven buildings, craft-making exhibits and paddle wheel boat rides on the Kentucky River. That sounds interesting. I'd love to see it." Amy's words trailed off as if she'd feared she'd just asked him for a date.

Unwilling to dampen what still had the potential to be a pleasant afternoon, Matt said, "It only takes about an hour to get there. You'd have plenty of time to explore the community on your day off."

"I think I will." Amy pushed her hand through her hair, obviously relieved Matt hadn't insisted on accompanying her on the excursion. When he turned south on Versailles Road, Amy said, "I assume we're picking the tour up in progress."

"Yeah, it actually starts downtown, but that's best to do on foot."

"Something to save for another day off."

Matt nodded. Though it was his nature to offer to escort her, he refrained from doing so.

Nearly two hours later, he hadn't seen Amy glance at her watch once. She'd oohed and aahed when they'd driven past the site of the original Calumet Farm, the Keeneland racecourse and a series of magnificent horse farms. Sometimes Matt slowed down as they passed by grazing horses or a historic cemetery and church, while other times Amy grabbed his arm and insisted they stop. She read the map aloud, offering tidbits he didn't know or had long forgotten. "Did you know locals believe Manchester Farm was the inspiration for Tara in *Gone With The Wind?* Did you know plank fencing costs eighteen thousand dollars a mile before painting? Did you know the American Saddlebred horse is the only native Kentucky breed?"

As they headed toward Aunt Lila's, Matt took pleasure in Amy's contented countenance. The afternoon had been a success. Amy was falling in love with his Kentucky.

"There's just one thing I don't understand," she said. With the sun behind them, she removed her sunglasses.

The bright wonder in her eyes nearly took his breath away. He had to swallow hard before he could ask, "What?"

"Why isn't bluegrass blue?"

Matt smiled at the question tourists often asked. "In the early spring you'll find small blue blossoms on the grass. From a distance the pastures look like a blue-green sea."

"I see," Amy said, as if he'd just solved one of life's great mysteries.

Feeling playful, Matt reached out and squeezed her knee slightly. "One afternoon doesn't make you an expert on Lexington history."

"I bet I now know more about the city than a lot of people who've lived here their entire life."

"That's probably true," Matt said.

When their smiles faded, Amy looked directly at

him and said, "Thanks for making this a special afternoon. I really enjoyed myself."

"I had a good time, too," he said, stopping himself from suggesting they do it again soon even though he liked Amy and enjoyed her company.

But there wasn't any magic between them.

Even though he didn't believe in love at first sight, he'd always thought that when he met the woman God meant for him to share his life with, he'd know it. He'd feel a click in his soul. And then together, they'd slowly fall in love as their friendship and trust deepened. This time spent with Amy had convinced him she wasn't The One. While he found her beautiful and alluring and easy to get along with, he hadn't felt that undeniable click. And more important, he could tell she didn't feel any magic, either.

By the time they reached Aunt Lila's, he felt an odd mixture of relief and disappointment. Was he ever going to meet the woman of his dreams? He opened Amy's door and took her hand, and when he looked into her eyes the pain and confusion he saw riveted him. She was a wounded soul, and his heart ached for her. He'd had every intention of keeping his distance from her in the future, but now he knew he couldn't. It was because of his meddling that she'd accepted the job with Aunt Lila. He would help her rebuild her life. But not out of love. He would help her because he felt obligated.

Chapter Five

Because it was nearly dinnertime, Amy wasn't surprised to see Matt cross the lawn on his way from the stable to the house. His morning and evening visits to check on the horses were as dependable as a quartz clock. On the occasions when their paths crossed, they kept the conversation light and simple. She'd ask if the new horse had settled down, and he'd assured her that with every passing day the mare was growing more accustomed to her new surroundings. When he asked if there was anything he could do to help her feel more at home, she said she was just fine, that the Lexington air agreed with her.

But even though they didn't say much, she felt his presence constantly. On most mornings, when she pulled the sheers aside to peer at the dawning sky, he would stop his work—whether he was riding in one of the corrals or passing through the barn's double doors—to smile at her and wave. When she passed him in the car on the long, winding driveway, she'd tap the horn lightly. And each night near dusk, while he sipped iced tea on the veranda with Aunt Lila, she busied herself in the kitchen. She'd only been at Lila's a little over a week, and already she gauged her routine by his.

But as long as he kept his distance she didn't mind. In fact, she felt safer when he was at the farm, though she'd never tell him that. Nor would she tell him the other confusing thoughts that still chased through her dreams. Though it had been ten days since the robbery, she could still feel his arms around her and hear him whisper, "Trust me."

In the darkest part of the night, his words echoed in her mind. *Trust me.* Yes, she had wisely trusted him in a moment of danger. But she wouldn't trust him, nor any other man for that matter, with her heart for a very long time. Garry, her ex-fiancé, had made certain of that. Everything would be just fine, she convinced herself, if she could keep Matt at a distance through the summer. She'd be his date to the three family weddings, and after thanking him for the thousandth time for saving her life, she'd leave this farm and never see him again.

Amy swallowed hard, taking a swig of water to wash down the unexpected twang. She liked Lila's farm. It would be difficult to leave this haven. By the end of the summer, though, it wouldn't seem as scary, she convinced herself. By then she'd have secured a new job and she'd be back on her feet ready to face the world with God at her side.

Squatting with her back toward the stables, she surveyed the newly planted row of basil, pretending she hadn't noticed Matt. As she pushed moist soil around the tender stems, she prayed Matt would pass by the garden without a glance her way, check on Lila, who was napping, and then go home without bothering her. Near her bare feet lay the cellular telephone in case Lila needed her, a jug of ice water and a small radio, which she had tuned to a classical station.

"Somebody's been working hard," Matt said.

Even though she'd half expected his approach, she still jumped.

"Didn't anyone ever tell you it wasn't polite to sneak up on someone from behind?"

He nodded. "But I didn't sneak up on you."

She started to deny she'd seen him leave the stable, then decided it was futile. "I didn't expect you to detour through the garden. I figured you'd be in a hurry to get home. You've stayed late every night this week."

Desperate to avoid meeting his gaze, Amy dropped to her knees and began planting the flats of thyme and parsley. Carefully pulling the root balls from the nursery containers, she nudged the young plants into the holes she'd dug and fertilized. Following Lila's instructions, her first attempt at gardening had gone smoothly. Until now. Until she'd opened her mouth and let Matt know she watched his comings and goings. But it was only because she wanted to avoid the man, to put some distance between them, that she even noticed his presence.

"I do spend a lot of time here," Matt said, bending to help her finish planting the herbs.

"Thanks, I appreciate the help, but it's not necessary. It won't take me long to finish up. Besides, I'm sure you're eager to relax." She smiled, hoping her attempt to get rid of him didn't sound obvious.

"Then Aunt Lila didn't tell you she's invited me to dinner?"

Amy shook her head as she desperately searched for a reason to excuse herself from the meal. She should have known something was up when Lila had asked her to fix a large casserole and then had joked about Amy working up a big appetite by dinner.

"She forgot to mention you'd be joining us," Amy said. "However, I fixed a chicken and artichoke casserole this morning, so it won't be any trouble to set an extra plate."

"Great." Matt rose, smacking the dirt from his hands. "I'll get cleaned up."

"Me, too," Amy said, as she planted and watered the last parsley plant. Matt reached out his hand, and she placed hers in his. As he pulled her to her feet, she couldn't help but meet his gaze. The concern she saw in his eyes surprised her. Was it possible he was spending more time at the farm because of her? Was he worried she wasn't settling in quickly enough? Maybe Aunt Lila had heard her wandering the house late at night and had told him. Just because he'd saved her life didn't mean he had to continue looking out for her. Only because she couldn't confirm her suspicions, she kept them to herself. For now.

"So you've noticed my comings and goings?" he said, as he helped her gather her gardening tools and supplies.

"Only because Aunt Lila mentioned just this morning that you'd been spending more time here than usual. Of course, she said she couldn't remember the last time the farm needed so much repair. She's worried you're working too hard." Amy put her own twist on Lila's comment.

"Not much gets past Aunt Lila. Though it looks like I'm going to be putting in extra hours for a while. The high school boy who helps me in the afternoons is grounded for the month."

"Grounded?"

"Apparently he's not doing too well in science, and he can't work until he brings his grade up in summer school."

"Can't you hire someone else to help out?"

"It'd be more trouble than it's worth." As Matt explained, Amy was drawn to the thoughtful glow in his blue eyes. He was a man who cared about others and wasn't afraid to get involved. She admired that quality in him. "By the time someone new learns the ropes, Billy will be back. So, until then, I'll do his chores. It'll be good for me. It'll keep me in shape."

If they'd been closer friends, she would have teasingly told him there was nothing wrong with his shape. Clad in his unofficial uniform of slim-legged blue jeans, a dark T-shirt and cowboy boots, he looked just fine. Yeah, he looked just about perfect.

Breaking through her ridiculous thoughts, she said,

"Billy's lucky to have such an understanding employer."

Matt removed his baseball cap, pushed his hands through his wavy hair and set the hat on his head. "Trust me, if the boy didn't remind me so much of myself when I was his age I wouldn't hold the job for him. I did make it clear that if he doesn't pass his next test I'll have to replace him. I won't have a choice."

"Well, did you ever think about selling a few horses?" she asked.

With the way his brows pushed together, she immediately knew she'd said something stupid. Then he cracked a smile, and she relaxed.

"You think I own all these horses?"

"Well... I..."

"Don't get me wrong, I'd love it if they were all mine. Most of them are boarded."

"Oh," Amy said. "I just assumed... I know how much you love this farm and the horses."

Matt's proud gaze swept over the corral, the line of stately barns and the chestnuts and bays slowly grazing across the bluegrass pasture. The clock tower on the main stable struck six o'clock, and chimes rang out across the Wynn property as they had for over a hundred years. As if to honor the generations before him, Matt waited until the Westminster Abby chimes finished sounding before continuing.

"I never had any intentions of boarding horses. It just happened. A friend of a friend wanted to buy a horse but needed a good stable. I've never advertised."

"Why not? If you love this land and your horses so much, why not make your living on the farm?" It seemed obvious to her. If he could do so well without a business strategy, just think what he could do with a plan.

Matt took a deep breath, digging the heel of his boot into the garden soil while he contemplated his answer.

"This is none of my business," Amy said, aware she'd asked something too personal.

Matt took his hat off and held it between his sturdy hands. "I don't mind the question. In fact, it's something I've asked myself more times than I'd like to admit."

"Then why don't you go for it?"

"Because the horse business is risky. It depends on the economy. When things are booming, I'd have no trouble filling the stalls. I could maintain a full schedule of riding lessons, as well as offering group trail rides and barbecues like other stables do. But when the economy is down, people don't spend money on horses."

"Are you telling me you're not a risk taker?"

Matt considered her question, then shook his head. "I just know what I want, and I know my accounting business is going to give it to me."

"But Lila said your biggest clients are somehow linked to the horse industry."

"True. But they're in the horse business for the

long haul. Plus, I've diversified my client base for stability.''

"And just what is it that you want that's so important?'' Amy asked. Matt shifted his weight from one foot to the other, then pushed his baseball cap over his head. It wasn't until he'd bitten his bottom lip that she realized she'd delved too deep. She wanted to stop him, to say, Don't tell me. I don't want to know those things that rest heavily upon your heart. I don't want to know too much about you. But it was too late.

"I want a wife and children. And I want to give them the same love and stability I've always known.''

Amy merely nodded. And in that moment she understood clearly why he'd asked her to be his date for three family weddings. Nearing thirty and still single, he was embarrassed to attend the weddings alone. Watching his cousins get married, seeing them embark on his dreams, had to disappoint him.

Amy knew she should say something encouraging, such as, It'll happen. Be patient. Love will find you when you least expect it. But she said none of these things, because she knew they weren't true. Love might sneak up on you, but only to break your heart. So instead, she said, "Love isn't everything they claim it to be.''

She saw the question forming on his lips and wished she had kept her cynicism to herself. But before he forced her to explain herself, her cellular telephone rang. Thank God for Lila. "Yes, we're coming in right now. Dinner's already made. It'll just take me a minute to heat the casserole and set the table.''

Closing the flip phone, Amy said, "We'd better not keep Aunt Lila waiting." Without hesitation, she hurried toward the house, eager to outrun Matt's dreams of marriage and family.

Matt grasped Aunt Lila's and Amy's hands as he said grace, thanking God for good food and family.

After taking a generous portion of the chicken casserole, steamed broccoli and warm wheat bread, he listened to Amy and Aunt Lila's friendly chatter. Amy had accused him of not taking risks, but he'd taken a huge risk when he'd brought her into his aunt's home. But as he listened to their warm exchange, he knew his instincts had been right. Amy was exactly what Aunt Lila needed. She helped without hovering, giving his aunt the assistance she needed without making her feel useless and dependent. And he could already see the changes in Amy. She smiled more often. She hummed when she didn't think anyone was listening. She felt more at ease around him. She'd proved that today when she'd made the comment about love.

He'd wanted to ask her what she meant. He wanted to know who had hurt her so deeply. But those were questions he couldn't ask today—maybe never. However, it wasn't important he know the source of her pain. What was important was that he help her rebuild her life. Help her get back on her feet so they could both move on with their lives.

"Your herb garden's looking mighty fine," Matt

said to Aunt Lila. "I predict you're going to have a bumper crop."

Lila smiled. "I knew Amy'd have the knack for gardening."

Amy set down her fork. "It's a little too early to congratulate me on a job well-done. Let's see if the plants are still thriving at the end of the month."

"Oh, I'm sure they will be," Aunt Lila said. "Herbs are just like anything else. All they need is a little sunshine, good nutrients and lots of tender loving care."

By chance, Matt met Amy's gaze and nodded at her unspoken question. Conversations with Lila were often layered with many meanings. Matt, along with the rest of his cousins, enjoyed his aunt's clever mind, except for the times when they were the target of her not so subtle messages.

After Amy's comment earlier about love not being all it was cracked up to be, he wasn't surprised when she redirected the conversation and inquired about Lila's plans for the next day. They would start with breakfast and a short walk. Afterward, Amy would help Lila pay bills and catch up on her correspondence. While Lila napped after lunch, Amy would run a few quick errands and then work in the herb garden.

Matt settled back in the chair and listened as the conversation came full circle and Lila began telling the old family story he'd heard hundreds of times.

"You see," Lila explained, her eyes bright with light, "Mary Todd Lincoln's family lived on West Main Street. Her father had remarried by this time, and her stepmother had a wonderful herb garden. She's the one who helped my great-grandmother start our herb garden.''

Amy smiled, nodded and said, ''Oh, my gosh,'' in all the right places. And with Amy's undivided attention, Matt knew Aunt Lila would talk well into the evening about the marvelous ways God had entwined the Todd and Wynn families. There were countless stories of how they'd helped and supported each other during times of tragedy as well as times of great happiness.

With nothing pressing to do at the office and no one waiting at home to welcome him with open arms, Matt was content to sit back and enjoy the evening. A warm June breeze snaked through the house, shadowed by the night sounds of crickets, cicadas and hoot owls. Helping himself to another glass of iced tea, he refilled Amy and Lila's glasses, too, topping each with a sprig of fresh mint.

Though he pretended to watch both women, Amy commanded his undivided attention. When she was distracted by Lila's tales, the sadness in her eyes retreated behind a smile that could have melted the heart of the bravest frontiersman. As she listened to the elder woman, Matt watched respect, admiration and genuine awe shape Amy's face. It occurred to him that if he wanted to know what his aunt had been like as a young woman he only had to look at Amy.

It was an interesting thought. Aunt Lila had always been an influential force in his life. Still, it was hard to imagine her as a wounded soul, uncertain in her faith and distrustful of love. Then glancing quickly from his aunt to Amy, Matt lost his breath as he glimpsed the woman Amy might one day become.

Her slender hand rested on the table, mere inches from his, and he fought the desire to reach out and touch her. He wanted to hold her as he had in the convenience store. He wanted to feel connected to her again as he had during those intense moments when their world had narrowed to a three-by-four-foot closet. But instead, he finished the rest of his iced tea in one gulp, wiping the sweat from his brow before anyone might notice his discomfort.

Thankfully, Aunt Lila brought the evening to a close with a big yawn and the announcement that it was past her bedtime. Matt kissed his aunt good-night, watched her leave the room and then knew he had to do something quick before he made a fool of himself with Amy. So he brought up the one topic that was certain to make her run.

"My cousin Susy's wedding is on Saturday."

"This Saturday?" Amy asked, her doe eyes looking everywhere but at him.

"Yeah, I can't believe Dave and Susy will be getting married on Saturday, either. This spring has flown by. It seems like only yesterday we celebrated their engagement. And that was six months ago."

Amy swallowed, bit her lip, then with steady eyes met his gaze. "Where should I meet you and at what time?"

"The wedding's at seven o'clock, and it's formal." She nodded as if to hurry him along. "Well, since

Aunt Lila's practically orchestrated this event on her own—which was no small feat considering she accomplished a great deal of it from a hospital bed—you probably know more than I do. Anyway, I thought I'd pick you up at six-fifteen.''

"That's kind of you, but not necessary. I'll be driving Lila to the church around the same time. We'll meet you—''

"I already promised Aunt Lila we'd all go together.''

"It's funny how these details seem to slip her mind.''

"Isn't it?'' Matt said, though he had a sneaky feeling his aunt's omission hadn't been by accident. Still, it was just as well, because despite the time he'd spent alone with Amy, she still seemed skittish about being his date to the wedding. "You know, if you don't want to go...''

Amy shook her head. "I'm just nervous about meeting your parents and sisters. Family gatherings can be a little overwhelming. At least mine always are.''

Though Matt believed she'd skirted his question, he didn't press her. She'd said she'd go to the wedding, and that was good enough. After all, this wasn't a real date, and there wasn't any pressure to impress her because he wasn't hoping something romantic would develop between them.

They'd go to the wedding and they'd have a nice time. It was that simple.

* * *

Matt had given her a graceful way out, and she should have taken it.

Though it was nearing midnight, Amy sat on the veranda in the hand-carved wooden rocking chair and watched the clouds pass over the bright moon. In the country quiet, she could almost hear God's voice telling her to stay, that to run would be a mistake.

Still, she was tempted to leave. It would only take a few minutes to load her few belongings into the trunk of her car. She could be miles down the highway before either Aunt Lila or Matt discovered she was gone. She'd never have to go to a wedding again. She'd never have to relive her own heartbreak and humiliation.

But Amy knew running wasn't the answer. She couldn't keep starting over. And after Lila's kindness, she could never leave the elder woman in a lurch. Standing, Amy wrapped one arm around a round column while leaning her cheek against the smooth white wood. Though she'd only been in Lexington a short time, she'd already fallen in love with the farm and under Lila Wynn's spell. Just being near the dear woman soothed her wounded heart.

She would stay, and as she'd promised, she'd help Lila though the summer, and she'd be Matt's date to three Wynn weddings. As hard as she knew it would be to walk into the church on Saturday and witness the promise of love between the bride and groom, she felt a deep peace and knew she was doing the right thing. Even though she'd appeared to have found the Wynn family by accident, she believed it wasn't a coincidence. No, it was all part of a bigger plan that she could neither see nor understand, but it required her to trust God.

And trusting God wasn't easy. Not after Garry's betrayal. Only a few months ago, as she'd been planning her own wedding, she'd been so certain she'd known God's plan for her life. Yet in this still, honest moment, she could admit that she'd never truly felt right about her engagement to Garry. She had wanted their relationship to work so badly that she'd tried to force her plans to fit into God's box.

As if to say He was listening, the chimes on the clock tower struck midnight. Mesmerized by the melodic phrases, Amy left the house and ventured toward the stables. Standing barefoot in the middle of the dewy lawn, she stared at the beautiful clock perched high atop the stable roof. It was simple in its design. The huge Roman numerals on the clock face were illuminated by bright spotlights. As the chimes continued, Amy recalled the family story Lila had told earlier in the evening.

"Great-grandfather Wynn commissioned the clock tower because he wanted to be reminded of God's caring hands whenever he saw the clock hands. And the ticking minute hand reminded him that God's timetable is not our own. He chose the Westminster chimes when he learned the words came from Handel's symphony. Lord through this hour, Be Thou our guide. So, by Thy power, No foot shall slide."

Though generations and years had passed, Amy

couldn't help but feel great-grandfather Wynn had built this clock tower just for her.

Closing her eyes, she listened to the twelve powerful chimes. Holding out her hand, she imagined God's hand clasping hers. Only with His help could she face her greatest fear—a wedding.

Chapter Six

Without warning, Aunt Lila's home became busier than Grand Central Station, and Amy quickly discovered that tradition wasn't to be stopped. Taking Amy aside one morning, Lila quietly explained how she'd always coordinated the family weddings. She wasn't going to let a doctor's orders come between her and her niece's happiness. When Amy realized there was no way she could change Lila's mind, her only choice was to appoint herself unofficial wedding coordinator.

Luckily, she had plenty of help as a constant flow of aunts, cousins and family friends came through the front door eager to help. Three days before the wedding, as all the Wynn brides had before her, Susy and her bridesmaids moved into the upstairs guest bedrooms. The grand old house overflowed with chatter, hugs and happy tears. Wedding presents began arriving on an hourly schedule. First neatly stacked on the dining room table, they soon overflowed into the formal living room. Everywhere Amy turned she saw shiny white paper and satin bows. The telephone rang continually. Florists, caterers, photographers and travel agents all needed approval on last-minute details. Though Amy tried to screen the calls, more got through to Lila than she would have liked.

Amy had never worked harder in her life, nor had she spent more time on the telephone. When an overwrought seamstress threw her hands up in frustration, Amy came up with the idea that saved the day. When the frantic caterer called for the final guest count, Amy added fifty to the confirmed RSVP list and crossed her fingers. It didn't take a genius to know the entire Wynn family would attend the wedding. And when the restaurant that was supposed to host the rehearsal dinner closed due to bankruptcy two days before the wedding, Amy won the bride's and Lila's undying gratitude by relocating the dinner and adding some surprises that were certain to make the evening extra special.

So it wasn't until after Lila left with one of her nephews for the rehearsal dinner and the house was quiet that Amy's nerves rebelled. For the past few days, she'd been trapped in a whirlwind of activity. By bedtime, she'd been too tired to think about her fears. She said good-night to God and then promptly fell asleep.

Even though Matt had spent twice his usual amount of time at the farm, she hadn't had a minute alone with him. There was always a family member underfoot. By the end of the week, she'd met his parents, his older sisters, all the aunts and uncles, the nieces and nephews, as well as many friends and neighbors. Though Amy stopped trying to remember names, they all seemed to know who she was, and they welcomed her into the family as if she were truly a Wynn. At first, she'd felt uncomfortable with their brand of hospitality, but in the end their warmth and friendliness had won her heart.

But now, all she could think of was her date with Matt.

Feeling restless, Amy couldn't seem to soothe her jangled nerves. She quickly grew tired of pacing figure eights around all the wedding gifts. She didn't have the patience to soak in a hot tub. She didn't want to go to a restaurant alone, nor was she in the mood for fast food. Going to the mall or a movie didn't interest her. As if her feet knew what was best for her, she soon found herself heading toward the top of Matt's hill.

Though he'd said he would share it with her, she hadn't ventured this high since the day she'd moved to the farm. She sprinted up the hill. It felt good to stretch her legs and breathe in the fresh summer air. In the approaching sunset, there was enough light to plainly see the dirt path, while golden hues that reminded her of royalty shadowed the trees, rocks, hedgerows and wildflowers.

She reached the summit and stopped to catch her breath. Below, the outer edges of Lexington twinkled as lights flickered on. Though she was alone, it wasn't quiet. Frisky squirrels and rabbits hurried through the underbrush. Birds chirped, urging their young ones to hurry home. And somewhere in the heart of the city, the Wynn family gathered to celebrate family love.

Though Susy and Dave had insisted she come to the rehearsal dinner, Amy had made an excuse to stay behind.

"We want you to join us," Susy had said. "You're like family. If you hadn't been able to take over for Aunt Lila this week, there wouldn't be a wedding."

Amy had hugged Susy and smiled at the exaggeration. "I'll see you tomorrow." And then Susy had been called away, and Amy had slipped upstairs until everyone had left.

Overwhelmed with her memories, Amy pulled the letter that had arrived in the afternoon mail from her pocket and clutched the lavender envelope. She didn't need light to read the note she'd already memorized. Her mother wanted her to come home. She thought Amy had had plenty of time to pull herself together, and now it was time for her to come back to Ohio and get on with her life.

Amy had tried to explain to her parents why she needed to leave Ohio, but in the end she'd given up trying. How could she explain something she didn't fully understand herself? Still, one thing had been clear on the morning she'd left her hometown. She couldn't bear to live in the same town as Garry and his new girlfriend.

For the past week, she'd managed to shove thoughts of Garry to the back of her mind. But here in the hilltop solitude, the anger, humiliation and resentiment seeped out. They coated her with a slime she couldn't wash off. They made her feel sluggish and uncoordinated. Powerless. She picked up a small stone and hurled it into the air.

Distracted by the Wynn family, she'd been lured into a sense of false security. Because she'd kept thoughts of Garry at bay, she'd believed she was healing, that she was coming to terms with what had happened. But as she doubled over in pain, she knew that wasn't the case. The hurt and anger ran as deep as they had the moment she'd caught Garry kissing her cousin.

She hated feeling like this, but she didn't know how to make the ugly emotions go away. She'd prayed and begged until she knew God was bored with her cries. Looking at the night sky, she shook her fists at God, then dropped to her knees on the hard dirt. Sobbing, she gave in to the helpless feelings, certain she was destined to feel this way forever.

How on earth was she ever going to survive tomorrow's wedding?

Matt escorted Aunt Lila to the car, then went to tell Amy it was time to leave for the church.

From the car, Aunt Lila called, "We've got plenty of time. Don't rush her."

Matt waved, signaling that he'd heard his aunt, then hurried into the house. Where could Amy be? Glancing at his watch, he noticed it was six-fifteen. Technically, she wasn't late. Still, he couldn't ignore the uneasy feeling that she wasn't going to show. That she'd packed her bags and run away.

And the only reason that bothered him was that Aunt Lila seemed so taken with the young woman, and he knew it would be next to impossible to persuade Lila to hire a replacement should Amy bolt. At least that's what he told himself.

He checked the downstairs first, rushing through the rooms that had been returned to their normal elegant state. The gifts and wedding decorations had all been moved to the church reception hall. No clues of the satin bows, mounds of presents or fragrant flowers that had been scattered across the room remained. Then Matt spied a lone carnation. A forgotten boutonniere. Picking up the white flower, he twirled it between his fingers. Someday, he'd be the one getting married. Someday, his dreams would...

Still holding the carnation, he stood at the bottom of the stairs and called for Amy.

"Amy," he yelled a second time when there was no answer.

Worried they'd be late, he started up the stairway two steps at a time. He was halfway up when she emerged from out of nowhere. Wearing a simple icy blue sheath with a matching silk cardigan and a single strand of large pearls, she stood at the top landing. He knew it was impolite to stare, but he couldn't help himself. She was beautiful—from her gorgeous legs to her nervous smile.

Finding his voice, he said, "It's time to go."

She seemed in no hurry to move. Then he remembered the boutonniere he held in his hand. Though the white carnation wrapped in baby's breath had been ordered for the men of the family, it somehow seemed fitting to give it to her since, she was his date.

When she took a tiny step backward, he met her on the top step and said, "I thought you'd like to wear this."

Though she hid her true emotions behind a tense smile, he knew she was pleased when she reached out to take the carnation. Like a fumbling idiot, though, he dropped the flower when his hand brushed against hers. Then when they both bent down to retrieve it, they came face-to-face, and he looked into the saddest eyes he'd ever seen.

Standing, he pinned the boutonniere onto her sweater, all the while inhaling her fresh scent as if he were a parched man secretly enjoying a sip of ice water. Then he grabbed her by the hand, as if it were the most natural thing in the world, and headed for the car.

The historic stone chapel sat on a small plot of land beyond the city limits, nestled in a patch of woods with brilliant wildflowers edging the front walk. Amy thought it was the perfect place for a cozy family wedding.

Taking a deep breath as she entered the church, she prayed for the strength to make it through the evening. When an usher offered his arm to Lila, Amy had no choice but to follow behind them with Matt. With her hand on Matt's arm, she felt surprisingly steady. Seated on the bride's side, the fourth pew from the front, near the wall, Amy tried to enjoy the beautiful organ music. But all she could think of was the wedding she'd planned for her and Garry.

It was to have been a simple affair with only family and the closest friends present. She would have worn her mother's gown with the endless train and carried a cascading bouquet of apricot roses and baby's breath as she promised to love, honor and cherish Garry for the rest of her life.

But then she'd seen Garry kiss her cousin Rhonda, and her whole world had changed. There had been a bitter fight, tears and angry words. In an instant, her heart, as well as her dreams, had been shattered.

As if Matt sensed her discomfort, he protectively stretched his arm along the back of the pew, his hand lightly brushing her shoulder. Caught up in her misery, Amy recoiled at his accidental touch. Though she felt his gaze upon her, she refused to look at him. There was certain to be comfort or sympathy in his warm blue eyes, and she didn't want either from him. In fact, she didn't want anything from him. Not even the friendship he seemed so willing to give.

Fidgeting in her seat, Amy yearned for the ceremony to start, for the sooner it began the sooner it would be over. Glancing over her shoulder, she noticed the chapel was nearly full. And for just a second, because of where she sat, she was able to catch a glimpse of the bride and her father as they waited in the far corner of the foyer.

Susy glowed in the antique lace gown. As the bride

looked at her father and smiled, Amy lost her breath, and tears threatened release. Suddenly there wasn't enough oxygen in the room, and the sanctuary walls felt as if they were going to fall upon her.

She had to escape.

She couldn't stay.

Thankful she sat near the aisle, she whispered to Matt that she had to use the rest room, and then without waiting for a reply she hurried down the aisle and out a side door. Just as she left the sanctuary she looked back and saw the first bridesmaid start down the aisle.

Staying to the right, she avoided the entryway, not wanting to disrupt the wedding party, and followed a hallway that led to a small fellowship hall. Halfway there, she saw the sign Women on a door and charged in. In the privacy of a stall, she let her tears flow.

The organist paused, and on cue Matt stood with the rest of the wedding guests as the bride appeared at the back of the church, standing beneath an arbor of pastel flowers. He'd never seen Susy look more radiant, nor his uncle Chad more proud. A reverent silence settled across the room, broken only by the young ring bearer's astonishment.

"Wow, Aunt Susy, you look beautiful," Luke called from the front of the church. The crowd chuckled, Luke covered his very red face with the ring pillow, and the organist hit her first note of "Here Comes the Bride."

Only after the bride had passed by his aisle did

Matt realize Amy had failed to return from the rest room. Nonchalantly, he searched what he could see of the entryway, but failed to catch even a glimpse of his date. Where could she be? Then the sinking feeling hit. She wasn't coming back.

He tried to tell himself he didn't care. She was a grown woman. If she hadn't wanted to be his date, she should have told him so. He wasn't so uncaring he'd force a woman to go out with him.

Nervously, Matt searched the back of the church one more time. Again, no sign of Amy. Growing tired of smiling at those guests seated directly behind him, he had no choice but to turn his attention toward the front of the church. As he watched Uncle Chad place Susy's hand in Dave's, he swallowed hard. He wanted what they had. And in a selfish moment, he couldn't help but cry out to God, *When will it be my time?*

It wasn't that he didn't wish Susy and Dave all the happiness in the world. He just wanted a little marital bliss to drift his way.

With dry eyes and her makeup refreshed, Amy hurried along the hallway to the back of the church. When she heard the loud, joyous organ music, she knew the wedding ceremony was over. Entering through a side door, she reached the back corner of the high-ceilinged entryway at the same moment the bride and groom burst into the room.

Filled with joy, Dave picked up his bride and twirled her around the room, her white satin train floating through the air. Susy let her head hang back, and her love-filled laughter echoed throughout the intimate chapel.

Amy inhaled deeply, too mesmerized to release her breath. Suddenly, she saw Garry's face in place of Dave's, and she imagined it was Garry whirling her through the air. It was Garry looking at her with love-filled eyes. In that instant, she recalled how easy it had been to fall in love with Garry. She remembered how he'd made her feel as if she were the only woman in the world. She remembered how he'd made her laugh. She remembered how nervous he'd been the first time he'd asked her out and how she'd blushed when he'd kissed her. He had a charisma she hadn't been able to resist.

Completing one last whirl, Dave eased to a stop. With Susy's feet firmly planted on the stone floor, Amy's trip down memory lane came to an abrupt halt. She bit down hard on her lip to contain the feelings of bitterness and anger as the rest of the bridal party emerged from the sanctuary and formed a receiving line across the back of the entryway. As she'd done so many times in the last few weeks, she carefully shoved her hurt and sorrow into a dark corner of her heart. This wasn't the time to deal with Garry's betrayal. There would be plenty of time when she crawled into bed to plead with God for help.

When Matt appeared in the doorway, she offered him an apologetic smile and slipped into the receiving line a step ahead of him. Not until he placed one hand firmly on her shoulder did she realize he feared she might bolt again.

Surprisingly, his touch steadied her nerves just as
it had while they'd huddled in the convenience store
closest. When his hand dropped protectively to her
waist, pulling her snugly to his side, she remembered
how perfectly their bodies had fit in the cramped
quarters. Compelled by his compassion, she glanced
at him, intending to communicate her appreciation,
only to be startled by the uneasy look in his eyes. He
hadn't been trying to soothe her nerves. He'd been
reaching out to ease his own discomfort. She placed
her hand over his and squeezed, just as she had as
they waited in the closet. Together, they'd get through
the wedding and reception. Together, they'd cast
aside their own selfish fears and celebrate with the
bridal couple.

Forcing a bright smile, Amy hugged and kissed
Dave and Susy and wished them all the happiness in
the world.

"Don't wish it all away," Matt whispered, as he
caught up to her.

"Wish what away?" Amy asked, as she started
down the steps. Washed and polished by years of
harsh weather, the stone felt uneven and slick beneath
her high heels. Without thinking, she reached out for
Matt's arm and found the stability she needed.

Across the churchyard, she spotted Lila with Matt's
parents amidst a boisterous family crowd. Catching
Amy's eye, Aunt Lila winked. Immediately, Amy felt
a blush burn her cheeks as the other family members
turned to look at her and Matt. And when they re-
sumed their animated conversations, she didn't need

to be a mind reader to know they were making untrue assumptions about her friendship with Matt.

"Don't wish all the happiness away," Matt said, reclaiming her attention. "Save some for us."

For us, Amy thought, willing for a split second to consider what it would be like if there were an *us.* To see Matt's smile and know it was just for her. To hear Matt whisper words of love for her ears only. To embrace his support and friendship. To become part of the Wynn family.

Then Amy's heel caught on a stone, and she stumbled to her senses. This time, she ignored Matt's outstretched hand and grabbed the wrought-iron railing. As she regained her balance, she silently reprimanded herself for giving in to such foolish thoughts. There was no *us.* Until she made peace with Garry's betrayal, she couldn't risk giving her heart to any man.

As they walked toward Lila, Amy kept a safe distance between her and Matt. Looking at the evening sky, she said a prayer of thanks that Lila would be riding with them to the reception.

Within seconds, those hopes were dashed.

"I'm not feeling up to the reception. Louise is going to take me home," Aunt Lila announced, patting her younger sister's back. "We haven't had a chance to catch up all week, so we're going to seize the moment." Looking directly at Amy, she added, "And don't worry about coming home early. Enjoy yourself. Louise is going to spend the night."

Amy smiled, knowing Lila's mind was made up. Still, she had no intentions of staying any longer at the reception than necessary. She'd make an appearance and then, feigning exhaustion, she'd convince Matt to take her home early. "I don't think it'll be a late night for me, either. The last few days have worn me out."

Ignoring Amy, Aunt Lila squeezed Matt's hand. "You show this girl a good time tonight."

"Don't you worry," Matt said.

But Amy did worry. Leaning against the passenger window, she pretended to be captivated by the passing scenery as they drove the short distance to the wedding reception. Once inside the large modern reception hall, Amy slipped away from Matt's side, mingling amongst friends and family of the bridal couple. For nearly an hour, she managed to keep one step ahead of Matt. And then, when they did sit down for dinner, she purposely participated in the table discussion, leaving no opportunity for any private talk with Matt.

After dinner was served and the bride and groom had been toasted and the cake cut, the bridal couple made their way to the dance floor. As Amy and Matt stood on the sidelines, she knew there would be no escaping his arms.

When the second song ended and Matt hadn't asked her to dance, Amy felt slighted. She'd been so certain he'd insist on dancing, and because she'd agreed to be his date, she wouldn't have any choice but to follow his lead.

By the end of the third song, she'd grown tired of watching the couples float by and turned to study his face. There was a look in his eyes, an expression on his face she couldn't read. When he pursed his lips, she felt as if he were engaged in a silent debate. Something obviously troubled him. And when he sensed her interest and their eyes met, she knew he felt the same conflicting emotions she did. One second she felt as if she were in the presence of an old and treasured friend, and the next second she realized they were nothing more than acquaintances.

Sensing Matt wasn't going to break the silence between them, Amy did the only thing she could to end the uncomfortable moment.

"Would you like to dance?" she asked. At least then she wouldn't have to look into his dark blue eyes.

Matt nodded, took Amy by the hand and led her to the dance floor. The song ended, and Matt and Amy stood on the crowded dance floor looking everywhere but at each other. Amy thought it seemed like forever before the band leader quietly called out, "One, two, three," and the next song began. Much to her dismay, the lights dimmed as the slow, romantic waltz began.

Amy swallowed repeatedly as she found herself inching closer to Matt with each turn on the dance floor. She blamed their closeness on the music, on the mood in the room and most importantly on the handsome man whose hand rested lightly on the small of her back. When she pressed her cheek against his shoulder, his hold on her tightened slightly. Just enough for her to know he liked the intimacy.

Closing her eyes, she relived the quiet moments in

the storeroom when it had been just her and Matt, their hearts beating as one. She'd thought what they'd felt then would diminish with time in the harsh light of the real world. But it hadn't. If anything, the bond she felt with this man had grown stronger.

But what was it she felt for him?

Was it merely gratitude for saving her life? Was it some kind of survivor bond? She'd read articles about strangers who'd relied on each other to survive crashes, earthquakes and floods, only to find themselves forever linked. Yes, it was that. But it was more, too.

Matt made her feel like a woman. He made her feel desirable. Even though she'd rationally known she wasn't at fault for Garry's betrayal, there was a voice in the back of her mind that had whispered she hadn't been woman enough to keep Garry. That if she'd been more attractive, more witty or more interesting, he wouldn't have strayed. And without meaning to, she'd twisted these thoughts around and around until she felt like she wasn't attractive to any man.

Amy sighed, feeling strangely comforted by Matt's embrace. And then it occurred to her that she'd been so caught up in her own concerns she hadn't considered what signals she might be sending him. By relaxing in his arms, had she unintentionally let him think she was interested in him? She wasn't. Not at all. While she found his attention flattering and even enjoyed his company, she wasn't attracted to Matt. At least not in that way.

Oh, God, she prayed. *What have I done now?*

With each turn on the floor, she pulled away from Matt until their only contact was the light touch of his hand on her back and their two hands pressed together near his shoulder. Only when they once again danced and moved with the awkwardness of strangers did Amy exhale.

Chapter Seven

Matt lost track of the other dancers on the floor. Swaying to the music with perfect rhythm, all seemed right with his world. Closing his eyes, he thought only of the woman he held in his arms and how wonderful it felt to be close to her again. Just as they'd been in the storeroom closet.

It had been almost a month since that eventful day, and he'd thought by now that the intense feelings that had been born in the darkness of the convenience store would have dwindled to nothing but an awkward silence. But that wasn't the case. When he was with Amy he still felt a puzzling connection. For reasons he didn't understand, whenever he was with her he felt the urge to tell her things he'd never told anyone else. He wanted to share his hopes and dreams with her. He wanted to see a sparkle in her eyes that said she understood his passions and felt the same way he did. And he wanted to know what she yearned and prayed for.

Moving across the dance floor as one, he couldn't help but wonder again if she were The One. Could she be the one who would end his lonely nights? The one he'd raise his children with? The one he'd look forward to growing old with?

The fantasy was easy to believe. And then he felt the shift in Amy. She stiffened and moved away from him as if he were contagious, as if she'd suddenly read his thoughts and couldn't bear the intimacy. He lost count of the beat, and his rhythm faltered, leaving him off balance and feeling foolish.

If she were the one, he would have known it by now. Deep in his heart, he would have felt an undeniable confidence. No, Amy wasn't the woman of his dreams. Yet he often dreamed of her at night. He was attracted to her, drawn to her, and the only explanation he could accept for the strength of these feelings was that God, for reasons He'd yet to reveal, had brought them together. And because he truly believed that if he turned his back on Amy he'd be turning his back on God, Matt wasn't going to let her slip away.

But for now, he let her take the lead on the dance floor. When the song ended, he whispered in her ear, ''Why don't we call it a night.''

Amy nodded, and taking her hand he led her through the crowd, saying good-night to family and friends as they made their way to the car. Though they rode back to Aunt Lila's in silence, Matt knew they had a lot to say to each other.

* * *

As Amy had expected, Matt walked her to the back door. When he lingered, she didn't have the heart to say good-night without apologizing for her odd behavior.

"I haven't been a very good date," she said, her head hanging low. "And I'm sorry."

"Hey, there's nothing to apologize for," Matt graciously insisted. Using one finger, he lifted her chin in order to meet her gaze. "First dates are awkward enough. You should have had your head examined for agreeing to go with me to a family wedding. That's like asking for a double dip of trouble."

"Me? Have my head examined?" Amy laughed quietly so as not to attract Aunt Lila's and Louise's attention. As she'd approached the house, she'd noticed the women's silhouettes. Near the fireplace in Aunt Lila's upstairs sitting room, the two sisters had been so engrossed in conversation they hadn't even turned their heads at the sound of car doors slamming. "What about you? This date was all your idea."

"Thank you for reminding me." Matt shook his head with disbelief. "At least the wedding went off without a hitch, and Dave and Susy are happily married."

"It was a beautiful wedding," Amy said. Then glancing away, she added, "At least, what I saw of it."

Maybe because Matt didn't pry, Amy felt compelled to explain. "I made an excuse to leave the chapel," she said.

"You don't owe me any explanations."

"I think I do." Raising her head, she dared to look directly into his dark eyes, and when she did, the compassion she saw convinced her he would understand her turmoil.

But before she could say any more, he said, "It's still early. Why don't we take a moonlight horse ride?"

Amy smiled, momentarily off the hook. "That sounds like a great idea, except for one thing. Remember...I don't ride."

"Luckily, that can be remedied. I know a very good instructor. In fact, he can teach you to ride in a weekend."

"That's generous, but not necessary." However, Amy knew he wasn't going to let go of the notion. He was too much like his aunt. Once an idea took root, he didn't veer from his course.

"Are you kidding? You can't live on a horse farm in Lexington and not know how to ride. That'd be like living on an island and refusing to learn to swim. It wouldn't be natural."

"Okay, sign me up. But for tonight, can we keep our feet on solid ground?" The words instantly rang as an ominous warning in her heart. She couldn't let her guard down with this man for an instant lest he find his way into her heart.

"A walk it is," Matt said.

"Let me change my clothes. I'll only be a minute."

Alone in her room, Amy carefully unpinned the carnation and set it on the dresser before stripping and pulling on jeans, a T-shirt and walking shoes. Though she quietly glided through the house and left without disturbing Lila and Louise, she doubted her presence had gone unnoticed. Few things escaped Lila's knowing eye.

The path was easy to follow in the bright moonlight. Against the black sky, the stars swirled like a Van Gogh painting, providing an ancient map to the top as Matt and Amy wound up the wooded hillside. They walked without talking, feeling comfortable in nature's symphonic silence.

Halfway to the top, Matt slowed. "Do you need to catch your breath?"

"I don't, but if you need to we can rest." She knew he'd take the challenge, and they continued up the hill. At the top, she did have to catch her breath, but not from the exertion of the hike. Though she'd seen this view before, the loveliness and grandeur still overwhelmed her. And just for a moment, she felt as if she could reach out her hand and touch the heart of God.

And then the moment passed.

But she didn't despair. Instead her confidence rose. She felt certain that in time she would make her peace with God here on this mountaintop.

Suddenly realizing Matt wasn't at her side, Amy turned to look for him.

"Over here," he called. Across the plateau, he perched on a large boulder. "Let me give you a hand."

Bracing his feet against a natural ridge in the rock,

Matt reached down, offering a secure hand to Amy. Placing her hand in his, she took a huge upward step, letting his strength pull her to the top. After only three steps, she came face-to-face with him at what felt like the top of the world. Because he didn't move, she had no choice but to remain in his loose embrace at the edge of the boulder.

In the soft moonlight, his eyes reflected warmth and safety. As she had in the storeroom closet, she found herself trusting him, feeling protected in his arms despite the dizzying height. He wouldn't let her fall. Without breaking his gaze, he pushed a strand of hair from her face, tucking the shiny locks behind her ear. Amy swallowed hard, absently turning her lips inward to moisten them with her tongue. Matt's head gradually tilted toward her, and she inhaled loudly, believing he wanted to kiss her.

Matt froze, then pulled away, drawing Amy with him to the center of the boulder. Though she felt a sense of relief, she also felt an unexpected wave of attraction and found her traitorous mind wondering how Matt's kisses would have made her feel. Would they have made her knees shake so badly she couldn't stand? Would they have made her heart beat so loudly the whole world could hear it? Would they have tasted like honey, luring her into wanting more of his sweetness?

"A penny for your thoughts," Matt said. Just a foot away, he sat on the boulder. Amy joined him, keeping a comfortable distance between them.

"A penny?" she said, determined to inject a shot

of lightheartedness into the conversation. "You can't afford my thoughts. Besides, they're not for sale." At least, not her thoughts about kissing him.

"Then I guess I'll just have to rely on my own assumptions."

While the mischievous grin and playful look in his eyes convinced her he was teasing, she was afraid he'd already made some wrong assumptions. And that was her fault. Before they left this hilltop tonight, she'd make sure Matt Wynn understood she wasn't interested in anything beyond friendship.

Playing his game, she asked, "And what assumptions would those be?"

"Let me see," Matt said, scratching his chin. "That you're beautiful and intelligent."

"Not bad. Care to keep the winning streak alive?"

Matt studied her face, as if her eyes or smile might reveal something he hadn't noticed before. "I see a woman with guts and perseverance."

Amy shifted on the hard rock. "Well, that would be debatable. My friends and family back home would say I tend to overreact and take unnecessary risks."

"It's all in the eyes of the beholder."

"And which side you're looking at the truth from," Amy added. With that thought came an even more disturbing thought. She'd been so quick to judge and condemn Garry when she'd caught him kissing another woman. Though he'd tried to explain, she hadn't really listened. Was it possible things weren't as they had seemed? Obviously, he'd betrayed her love, but were there circumstances and misunderstandings that had led to this breach? Had things been going wrong between her and Garry for longer than she'd been willing to admit? Was this the only way he'd known to tell her it was over between them?

Amy shivered. Though what Garry had done was wrong, perhaps she'd been to blame, as well. But she didn't want to think about that now. Not on this beautiful summer evening when she had the world at her feet.

"Here," Matt said, removing his suit jacket and draping it over her shoulders. She smiled, though she wasn't cold. Yet, once she felt the weight of the fabric, she didn't want to give it back. Inhaling deeply, she savored Matt's woodsy scent and instantly relaxed.

"If I was you, I'd quit while I was ahead," Amy prodded.

"Not on your life. I know so much about you, it'll take all night to list the many mysterious aspects of your personality."

"So now I'm a woman of mystery."

Matt smiled, as if he held a few secrets himself. Then taking her hand in his, he rubbed her palm as if it were Aladdin's lamp, then turned her hand over several times.

"And what great mystery do you see now?" Not only had he captured her curiosity, but she found she was enjoying this interlude. Seeing herself through his eyes was fascinating.

In an authoritative voice, suggesting he was about

to reveal something profound, he said, "I feel a woman's hands. They are rough and blistered from recent gardening. Yes, definitely, this woman is new to hard labor. She's been pampered and adored her entire life."

Amy yanked her hand away. "Give me my hand back," she teased. "Your credibility just took a nose-dive."

"Oh, yeah?" he challenged.

"Yeah," she echoed, amused by the sparkle in his eyes.

"Then how about this," he said, taking her hand back and pressing it against his heart. "This is the hand that trembles at the thought of a wedding."

Amy tried to jerk her hand free of his clutch, but he held on tight.

"I didn't mean to hurt you," he said, his voice suddenly turning serious.

"I started to apologize earlier," she said, as he released her hand. She looked over the valley, and her voice felt as distant as the twinkling lights below. "I really thought I could handle the wedding, but I was wrong. It got to me."

Though Matt didn't touch her, he angled his body, bringing them closer together. "I'm guessing someone's hurt you. Someone you loved enough to marry." The concern in his voice left no doubt the game was over.

"I loved him," she said.

"He's the reason you left Ohio, isn't he?"

Amy searched Matt's eyes hoping to find a reason

not to trust him, not to confide in him. She'd had no intentions of ever telling him her secrets, but here on this hilltop she was overwhelmed with the desire to talk about the warring emotions that resided in her heart.

Before she knew it, the whole story came spilling out. How she'd known Garry since high school. How she'd loved him for years and had believed with all her heart he was the man God had destined for her to spend the rest of her life with. And how she'd caught him kissing her cousin.

"It was awful," she said. "It was bad enough that we broke up, but the wedding was only a few days away. We'd received gifts. My parents had made nonrefundable deposits to caterers and photographers.

"This didn't hurt just me and Garry. He betrayed them, as well. They'd opened their hearts to him and had welcomed him into the family as a son."

"I'm sure your parents were understanding. I can't believe they would have wanted you to go through with the marriage."

Amy pressed her hands against the side of her head and shook it lightly as if she could rid herself of all the painful memories. "At first they did, because they didn't truly understand what happened. Then after the dust had settled, they didn't trust my judgment any more than his. They started to take over my life, making decisions for me. I know everything they did was out of love and concern. They hated to see me so hurt. And maybe I overreacted, but I was afraid that if I let them take charge—which really would have been the easy way out—that I might never be able to regain control of my life."

Matt listened without interrupting, and when Amy finally paused long enough for him to get a word in he didn't say anything. Instead, he simply draped his arm across her shoulders and pulled her against his chest. For a long while they sat in the healing silence. Though nothing was said, much was communicated by the firmness of his hand on her shoulder and the evenness of his breath. He understood what no one else had seemed to grasp. There were no absolute answers. There were no easy fixes. It would take time for her to untangle the bitterness and hurt that strangled her heart. It would take time for her to approach God with confidence. It would take time for her to excavate a new path in life. And in his silence, Matt seemed to say, I'll be here for whatever you need. I believe you can make it through this hard time.

Finally, Matt said, "I'm sorry I put you in an awkward situation. You should have told me you didn't want to go to the wedding."

Amy pursed her lips. "Deep down I knew I needed to go to your cousin's wedding. I needed to face my fear. And if I hadn't wanted to repay your courage at the convenience store, I never would have considered going.

"But I did go. And I survived. I feel like I've fallen off a horse and been forced back into the saddle. But even so, I won't be planning another wedding any time soon," she added. She wanted him to be clear on that. She appreciated his understanding and compassion more than he could know, but she didn't want him to confuse her interest with attraction. No, there was nothing romantic between her and Matt.

"It'll be a long time before I fall in love again— if ever," she added for extra security.

"Never say never," Matt said.

"Oh, this is one thing I can be certain of."

Feeling she'd revealed more than she'd intended about herself, Amy was eager to redirect the conversation. "So, what about you? How come you had to ask a virtual stranger to be your date?"

"That's a long story," Matt said, suddenly feeling as if he were sitting on the hot seat.

"The night is still young, and I don't have anywhere else to go," she said.

"I was afraid of that. Besides, it's not much of a story." He hoped she would let the matter drop, but after the way she'd opened up to him, he doubted she would.

"That intrigues me even more. Of course, I could make my own assumptions."

Matt grinned. "I deserved that. But who knows, maybe you can read me like a book. That's what Aunt Lila claims."

"If anyone can see clear through a person's heart, it's your aunt. I've never met anyone like her." Amy's voice held bundles of respect and awe for the older woman.

"Now you've sparked my curiosity. Just what assumptions have you made about me?"

"Let's see," Amy said, as she rolled her eyes.

"You're a people person. Your family and friends mean a great deal to you."

"Go on," he said.

"You love horses and this land."

"You're not spilling any great secrets," he said. "I'll bet the mailman knows me this well."

"Okay," she said, scratching the soft spot behind her ear as she searched her mind. "You're a dreamer. You've got hopes and plans that you've never shared with anyone else."

"You're getting warm."

Placing her hands on either side of his face and looking deep into his eyes, she pretended to read his mind. For a moment his plans for the future shuffled through his head, only to be overshadowed by the tender touch of her gentle fingers. Her hands felt warm and caring against his cheeks, and he longed to cover her hand with his, then draw it to his lips where he would kiss away all her hurt and pain.

Though she'd stirred these romantic feelings deep within him, he knew that was not her intention. She'd made it clear she wasn't interested in him. And he wasn't interested in a relationship with her, either. She wasn't the woman God had chosen for him.

No, she definitely wasn't the one. It was odd, but knowing that released something within him. It made him feel free to share his heart with her. He knew he could trust her to be respectful of his dreams, and yet he didn't have to worry what she thought of them because she was never going to be a part of his future.

Amy pursed her lips, letting her hands slide from

his face. A small smile escaped her lips as she said, "I see a man who dreads going to weddings as much as I do."

Matt couldn't help but laugh. "Aren't we a pair?"

"I guess we're lucky we bumped into each other at the convenience store." Amy met his gaze as she spoke, and for just a second he felt the odd connection they'd felt in the storeroom. Only here on the hilltop, there were no walls to imprison them. They were free to go their separate ways.

"Maybe it was more than luck," he ventured.

"You mean that God meant for our paths to cross?"

Matt shrugged. "You do have a place to live and a job, and I've got a date to three family weddings."

Amy's eyes sparkled. "I guess when you look at it that way, we can't help but be friends. But don't think just because we're friends I'm going to let you off the hook. You never did tell me why you asked me to be your date."

Matt groaned, hoping she'd drop the embarrassing issue. "It's a complicated matter," he said.

"Give me a try," she said with a wide grin.

"I think you're enjoying this a little too much."

"And I think you're trying to avoid the question."

As he gathered his thoughts, Matt gazed toward the timeless horizon as if his future might be hidden in the maze of bright stars. Between the moonlight and the city lights, he could distinguish the houses in the valley below from the backdrop of low-rising hills and the faraway city skyline.

Biting his lip, he struggled to put his thoughts in order. "Ever since I was a kid, I've loved this spot. My granddad and my dad used to bring me here. I still feel their presence when I'm here. And maybe that's because a part of them will always be in my heart, and when I'm on this hilltop my heart is quiet enough to hear their voices."

He looked at Amy to see if she was bored, but when she nodded for him to continue he did. "I love this farm. I feel a connection to it that I can't explain. When I'm here I feel like I can have the past and the present and the future all rolled up in one."

"Wow," Amy said.

"But that doesn't really answer your question."

"No, but I'm trusting you're leading up to it."

Again Matt grinned. "I've always seen myself on this land. And my dreams have always included a family. Lots of children." He paused for a moment to swallow. "Yet, of all my cousins, by the end of the summer I'll be the only one not married. Not even a prospect in sight."

Amy's sigh of relief temporarily distracted him. "And in my family I can't show up at the wedding without a date. If I do, everyone's trying to fix me up, and I've had enough of their good intentions. Besides, when I've asked a woman I've only dated a few times to go with me it's awkward. It's too easy for her to get the wrong idea. You know, introducing her to my family and all."

"I see your dilemma," Amy said. "Well, it was

your lucky day when you met me. Because I'm the answer to all your dating problems.''

Matt nodded as the connection between them surged again. He couldn't help but think that meeting her had changed the course of his life. He'd just about given up hope of ever falling in love and getting married, and now...well, now it once again seemed possible.

"It's getting late," he said. "We should head back to the house."

"Otherwise, Aunt Lila might send a posse after us."

Matt held out his hand, and together they carefully inched down the side of the boulder. With the moon high in the sky and the path brightly lit, they quickly wound down the hillside through the woods. By the time they reached the edge of the formal garden, Matt noticed Amy's gait had slowed to match his. It was as if she hated for the evening to end as much as he did.

As she unlocked the wooden door, he held the screen door open. The lock released, and Amy pushed the heavy door forward. Turning to look at him, she said, "I had a really nice time."

"I did, too."

His gaze met hers, and they stood for what seemed like a long time in the haze of moonlight. He wasn't certain what he felt, and therefore he couldn't begin to guess what emotions lurked behind Amy's precious eyes. Across the lawn, the leaves of the grand oak and maple trees whispered in the gentle night breeze.

When Amy remained in the doorway, he knew he couldn't let this moment pass. Leaning forward, he hesitated, allowing her a chance to back away. Her breath felt warm on his cheek, and he longed to kiss her on the lips. But common sense intervened in the nick of time, and he pressed his lips against her forehead.

Backing away, he said good-night. Before she quickly hid her emotions behind a nonchalant smile, distrust and fear flickered in her eyes. "Good night," she whispered as she shut the door.

On the drive home, Matt chided himself for kissing her. Thank God he'd had the good sense not to kiss her on the lips. The more he tried to convince himself that he'd had to kiss her, that he'd had to know if she felt the same conflicting emotions he fought, the more he knew he'd made a mistake.

Her dark, troubled eyes haunted him. She was more vulnerable than he'd realized. From now on, she would be more careful around him. She wouldn't let her guard down again. Of that, he was certain.

It wasn't until he arrived home and sat in the driveway looking at his dark, empty house that he was able to face what worried him most. Closing his eyes, he prayed to God to help him make some sense of his emotions, to be able to separate his selfish desires from God's plan for his life.

As he prayed, he continued to see Amy's distrustful eyes in his mind. In that moment, he realized how much he cared about her. He could fall in love with her. Maybe even marry her.

Matt couldn't believe he was thinking such thoughts. He couldn't believe the terror he felt. His heart rate quickened, and a light sweat broke out across his brow. Squeezing the steering wheel with both hands, he tried to quiet his trembling.

In a moment of total honesty, he admitted to himself that it wasn't the thought of marrying Amy that scared him. It was the prospect of getting married in the near future that rattled him. As long as there had been no one special in his life, getting married seemed like a distant dream. But caring for Amy had pulled these dreams within reach. They were so close he could taste their sweetness.

For all he'd talked about getting married and raising a family, the thought of actually doing it scared him silly. He swallowed hard. He knew these feelings were related to what he'd recently seen happen to his close friends Gabe and Anna. Though he could name a dozen happy couples, he also knew the devastating heartbreak of a marriage gone wrong.

For now, he was happy to keep his dreams of a family untarnished. Until he was absolutely certain he'd met the one, he wouldn't even think about falling in love. The only chance a couple had of building a lasting relationship in this turbulent world was to be in a union blessed by God.

Feeling a measure of relief, Matt exhaled loudly and pushed Amy's image from his mind. He repeated what he'd been telling himself since he met her. That she wasn't the one. That God had brought her into his life to help her heal and get her life back on track. That was all, and nothing more.

Accompanied only by his idealistic dreams, Matt walked into his quiet house.

Amy closed the door quietly, then pressed her back against the hard wood. Crossing her arms over her chest as if she needed to protect her heart, she wondered how she'd gotten into this mess.

She was certain Matt wanted to kiss her.

Pressing her fingers against her lips, she wondered....

No, she couldn't follow those thoughts. If there was one thing she knew without a doubt it was that she wasn't ready or willing to trust a man's intentions.

And tonight had proved her point. Hadn't she made it clear she was only interested in friendship?

She wouldn't let that happen again.

Then she groaned. No, it couldn't be. Or could it? When Matt had talked of marriage and family, he couldn't have been thinking of her. But what if he did consider her bride material?

Though the idea seemed ludicrous, Amy couldn't ignore the possibility. From now on, she'd be more guarded. She'd keep her distance as much as possible. She'd make certain he understood the only thing she felt for him was gratitude.

Chapter Eight

Amy noticed a gradual change in Aunt Lila. Her pasty white skin went from pale to rosy as her energy level gradually grew. Yet, as Lila regained her health, Amy's job became more difficult. Because Lila felt just good enough to do too much, her doctor stressed that it was more important than ever for Amy to prevent Lila from becoming overtired. Which was next to impossible. Lila was restless. Having grown weary of her restricted and monotonous schedule, she was eager to get back to her old routines.

Dressing quickly in jeans and walking shoes, Amy hurried downstairs. Nearly a half hour had passed since she'd heard Lila stir, and she knew if she didn't rush, an impatient Lila would start off on her morning walk alone.

Luckily, Amy caught up with Lila just as she reached the backdoor.

"I thought I'd let you sleep in," Lila said. Wearing

navy shorts and a matching top, she looked as fit and trim as a woman half her age.

"I had plenty of rest, thank-you," Amy said. "Besides, you promised me last night you wouldn't wander off on your own again."

Amy had been frantic the previous afternoon when she'd come in from working in the herb garden to prepare dinner and had found the house suspiciously quiet. After a quick search, she realized Lila wasn't in the house. Using her cell phone, she found Lila relaxing on a bench near the corral watching as Matt exercised a mare.

"I don't know what the fuss is all about," Lila defended. "I'm only a cell phone away. That's why we bought these things."

"True. But you could have called me before you left the house."

"You're right," Lila conceded. "No more wandering off."

Well, the promise hadn't even lasted twenty-four hours. However, Amy couldn't help but sympathize with the woman's situation. She looked fine to Amy. Though no one in the Wynn family had come right out and said so, she suspected they all knew Lila was strong enough to manage on her own again. Still, they were genuinely worried about her living alone on this big farm, and they felt better knowing Amy was nearby at all times.

"We can hash this out while we walk," Lila decided.

Walking side by side, they followed their usual

route around the formal garden, no longer needing to stop and rest on the benches as they had when Amy had first arrived, and then following the perimeter of the lawn, down the driveway to the road and back to the house. Every day Lila walked a little farther and a little faster. Amy felt her own legs growing stronger and more agile.

"I feel like I'm treating you as a child, and I don't like that," Amy said as they passed the entrance to the formal garden where fragrant pink roses climbed wooden trellises as if to offer their gift of beauty to God.

"It's not your fault," Lila assured her. "You're only following my family's orders."

"And if you continue to refuse my help, then I'll have to look for another job and a place to live."

Lila came to an abrupt stop. "Oh, dear, we don't want that to happen. Unless you're not happy here."

Amy kept her smile to herself, pleased Lila had responded as she'd hoped.

"I've been very happy here." *In fact, maybe too happy,* she thought. Letting her gaze float across the beautiful landscape, she suddenly realized how difficult it would be to leave this farm at the end of the summer. How much she'd miss Aunt Lila and all the aunts, uncles and cousins that traipsed through on a regular basis. Yes, she'd even miss Matt.

"But that's not the point," Amy said. "You're paying me to do a job, and unless I do it, I'll have to go elsewhere."

"You drive a hard bargain," Lila said, starting to

walk again. "I'll be a better patient. I promise."
When Amy shook her head, Lila said, "Really."

With the matter settled, they walked a little way in
prayerful silence. This was the part of the day Amy
had come to look forward to. And on the few mornings she and Lila missed this prayer walk, the rest of
Amy's day felt unbalanced and misguided.

"I never could sit still long enough to finish a
prayer," Lila had told her on the first morning they'd
walked. "That's why I like to pray as I walk. I can
say a lot more to God this way, and I figure He
doesn't care whether I'm on my knees or on my
feet."

"I hadn't really thought about it," Amy said.

With each daily walk, Amy learned a little more
about the power of prayer.

"It's more than just talking to God and telling Him
your troubles or someone else's needs. You have to
stop and listen to Him. Otherwise, it's just a one-sided
conversation." Wisdom borne of experience shone
like a bright beacon in Lila's eyes.

"And there's nothing more useless than a one-
sided conversation," Amy said. She'd gone to church
for most of her life, and yet in a few short weeks
she'd learned more about having a relationship with
God than she ever had before. "But how do you
know when you've heard Him?"

She believed she heard God when she prayed about
whether or not she should marry Garry. She'd been
so certain God had brought them together and had
blessed their future. But now she had to wonder if

she'd only heard her own desires ricochet off the walls of her heart.

Garry was all the things she'd wanted in a husband. He was charming and fun, and she'd thought he shared her beliefs in God. But in the end, it didn't matter whose voice she'd followed, because Garry wasn't the man she was going to marry.

"Who knows what the voice of God sounds like." Lila attempted to explain. "I've never heard Him speak. At least not audibly. I think the word *knowing* is more accurate. When the thought or idea is from God it resonates with an authority in your soul as no other can. You know it in here." Lila thumped her fist over her heart. And when Amy looked at her with uncertain eyes, Lila added, "I wish I could explain it better. But I'll promise you this, if you'll take time to walk with God every day, you'll feel His presence in ways you can't deny."

As Lila spoke, an image of a younger Amy sitting on her father's lap while he dozed after a hard day's work flashed into her mind. With ease, she recalled the way his love had protected her and defined her place in the world. It hadn't mattered that they sometimes didn't speak. What had mattered was that they spent time together. Years later, she could still feel her father's love reaching out across the miles. Maybe God's love was like that.

Smiling at Lila, Amy said, "I'll take you up on that promise. I want to find God in the ways you have."

"The path is there, darling," Lila assured her.

"But yours is a little cluttered. It's going to take some time and energy to clear the way. You can't have a clear signal when there's static in the air."

Amy was still digesting Lila's last comment when she added, "I spoke to your mother last night." With a silent glance Amy asked how she could have missed hearing the telephone ring.

"You were in the shower, and your mother said she'd call back today," Lila explained.

"I'll try her when we get back to the house." Amy wondered if something was wrong but decided it couldn't be urgent or her mother would have insisted on talking to Amy last night. Until now, Amy had always called home. But lately, she'd let the time between her calls stretch into days because her parents asked too many questions she wasn't ready to answer.

"I can tell she misses you," Lila said with gentleness.

Though Amy didn't feel as if Lila were trying to pry, she did sense the elder woman offering her a chance to talk if she needed a sounding board.

"I miss her, too," Amy said. Yet not enough to go running home.

"If you'd like to invite them to visit, you're more than welcome," Lila offered. "There's plenty of room. Well, except Fourth of July weekend. Only Tam would plan a wedding on a major holiday."

"I assume the bridesmaids will be moving into the house before the wedding as they did at Dave and Susy's wedding?" Amy said, nudging the conversation astray.

Lila nodded proudly. "It's a Wynn family tradition that goes back three generations."

"And it's a lovely tradition."

When Aunt Lila grew suddenly silent, Amy realized she was thinking of how many Wynn traditions revolved around this farm and whether they would outlive her.

"Matt won't let your traditions end," Amy assured her.

"He's always appreciated the past, and I'm sure he'll marry a woman who'll embrace our family history." Lila's eyes sparkled at the thought.

It wasn't until they'd nearly reached the house that Lila managed to bring the conversation back to Amy's mother.

"Don't forget to call your mother," she reminded Amy.

"Thanks." Amy met Lila's eyes briefly, but in that split second she felt as if her friend sensed the root of her worries. But that was impossible. She hadn't confided in Lila about Garry's betrayal or the wedding that had been called off at the last minute or her fear of ever trusting her heart to a man again.

Yet Amy couldn't shake the feeling that Lila truly understood the jungle of emotions she struggled to work through. Daring to meet Lila's gaze again, Amy felt the strangest sensation. It was as if she were looking into the eyes of a younger woman. A woman who had made the same mistakes as Amy. A woman who'd felt the same heartache. A woman who'd survived the most confusing times.

Ever since she'd met Lila, Amy had seen her as the woman she was today. She hadn't considered what Lila might have been like before she'd married. Until now. And with those thoughts, hope rose in her chest. She swallowed hard and pressed her lips together, then thanked God for sending such a wise woman to be her example.

Amy's cellular telephone rang, interrupting her thoughts. She glanced at Lila. "It must be a wrong number. You're the only one who has this number."

Lila smiled apologetically. "I did give it to your mother last night...and to Matt."

Tempted not to answer, Amy let the telephone ring a few more times. But when Lila's intense stare turned to disapproval, Amy conceded.

"Hello," she said hesitantly.

"It's Matt. I hope I didn't catch you at a bad time."

"Actually, I was just helping your aunt." Before she finished the sentence, Lila waved and disappeared into the house.

"Then I'll keep this short. I was thinking about those riding lessons I promised to give you." he said.

"Don't give them a second thought. I know you're swamped until your helper can come back to work." *Please, please,* she said silently, *don't press me on this.*

"That's the good news. Billy got his grades back on track, so my workload has eased up."

"That's wonderful...for you and Billy," she said. In the distant pasture, a sleek horse stopped grazing, raised his head high in the air and then neighed. Amy smiled at the bay's timing. It was as if the horse were saying, "Come on, give me a try. Wouldn't you like to gallop across the pastures with the wind in your face?"

The old girlhood dream slipped to the surface of her mind and tantalized her. During her childhood, she'd gone through a phase where she'd read every novel she could find about a girl and her horse. But there'd been no riding stable near her suburban home, and eventually the dream had been cast aside.

So if she ever was going to learn to ride, this was her chance. And what was stopping her? The thought of being alone with Matt? She was silly to let that trouble her, because it didn't matter how Matt might feel about her, no man was going to woo his way into her heart. Not even a man with a horse.

"All right," she finally said. "I'll meet you at the stables on Saturday morning. What should I wear?"

"Aunt Lila will help you with that. She should have some boots and jodhpurs that'll fit you."

"Okay. I'll see you at eight."

Amy ended the call and sighed. She was going to learn to ride a horse.

"Whoa, Faith," Matt said, speaking confidently but softly to the sleek black horse. "Everything's fine. Steady, now."

Faith continued to nod, shifting her weight restlessly. Not until Matt inhaled the heavenly floral scent did he realize why his usually gentle horse had developed an instant case of the jitters.

Matt glanced over his shoulder just as Amy rounded the far corner of stalls and started toward him. Wearing tan jodhpurs and dark boots borrowed from his aunt, Amy looked comfortable in the equestrian wear. Not to mention attractive.

Faith whinnied her official welcome as Amy approached. Stroking the side of Faith's neck, Amy talked to the horse in a warm, friendly voice, which instantly calmed the horse. Just as he'd sensed Aunt Lila and Amy would be a perfect fit, so too were Faith and Amy.

"She's beautiful," Amy said. "What's her name?"

"Faith. Leap of Faith." Matt watched Amy closely, hoping for confirmation that it was love at first sight between Amy and Faith and that Amy wasn't just going through the motions of learning to ride because she was too nice to say no.

"Leap of Faith," Amy repeated. "I like that. Is she yours?"

Matt nodded.

"Is there a story behind her name?" As if on cue, Faith nodded her head once for yes.

Matt grinned. "She's got a mind of her own. Kind of like someone else I know."

Amy smiled back, then punched Matt lightly on the upper arm. "I'll take that as a compliment."

"As it was intended. She's a Morgan—" Matt started to explain.

"Justin Morgan Had A Horse," Amy interrupted.

Matt absently pushed his brows together as he tried to figure out why the phrase sounded so familiar.

When he failed to place it, he met her gaze and shrugged as if to ask her what she was talking about.

"Run, Appaloosa, Run," she said, as if it were a clue.

Matt shook his head.

"Wow, and you call yourself a horseman. You never heard of those two movies?" When Matt shook his head, Amy continued. "They're old, but they happen to be among my favorites. You know it's every girl's dream to have her own horse."

"Well, sometimes dreams come true. Because as long as you're here, Leap of Faith is yours to ride anytime you'd like."

When Amy's eyes widened revealing an equal blend of surprise and delight, Matt felt a funny thump in his chest. Teaching Amy how to ride wasn't going to be as easy as he'd thought it would be. And not because he doubted she'd be a good student. No, the problem was that he couldn't quit thinking of how perfectly she fit in his arms. First when they'd hidden in the closet during the robbery, and then later, when they'd danced at his cousin Susy's wedding.

Right now, if he could have plucked a good excuse out of the air, he would have pulled Amy into his arms. He wanted to smell the fresh scent of her hair and run the back of his hand down the side of her face. He wanted to banish her most vulnerable secrets and shine a light on her darkest fears.

Matt bit down on his bottom lip, momentarily returning his full attention to Faith. Though he'd been attracted to other women, he'd never felt anything as powerful as what he felt at this moment for Amy. Taking a deep breath, he grabbed hold of his senses. A man of values, he wasn't one to act on impulse. And that's all these feelings were, physical impulses. Without love, trust and friendship, these stirrings were nothing more than meaningless temptations. It was best he pushed them from his mind, because he and Amy were never destined to be more than friends.

When he realized Amy had asked him a question he hadn't heard, he blushed. Guessing she'd asked him again how Faith had gotten her name he said, "Her mother was in the middle of a difficult pregnancy when I purchased her. Everyone told me she was a risky buy, but I just knew she and her foal belonged here." Turning to Amy, he said, "You know that kind of feeling that burrows deep into your heart and won't let go?"

Amy nodded as if she understood, yet he saw the doubt in her eyes. "I've learned it's not wise to always trust those feelings," she said.

"We can't always be one hundred percent right. But think of all we'd miss in life if we never followed our hearts."

Before Amy turned away from him, he glimpsed her damp eyes and knew she was thinking of her ex-fiancé. Feeling a pang of jealousy, he told himself it was ridiculous to feel possessive.

"Hey," Matt said, putting his arm on Amy's shoulder and turning her toward him. When he saw the anguish in her eyes, a swift pain pierced his heart. "I'm sorry I've upset you."

"It's not your fault. And rationally, I agree life shouldn't be lived in fear. That we should take risks. But sometimes those risks require too much, and we have to take extra measures to protect ourselves."

Matt nodded. "But don't you see, I think you followed your heart here. Working for my aunt is no great career move. From the moment you stepped foot on this land, you knew God had brought you here to heal your heart."

Amy cocked her head to the right as she listened. Then a small smile escaped her lips. "I guess you're right."

"And what better place to put your worries behind you than at this beautiful farm?"

As if irritated by the lack of attention, Faith whinnied. Matt and Amy both laughed.

"Let's have some fun."

"Sounds like a plan to me," Amy said.

"Now that you've met Faith, let's get down to business."

If Amy had known learning to ride a horse was going to take so much energy, she might not have been so eager to mount Faith. Yet the first time she rode across the meadow, she knew it had been worth every aching muscle and sleepless night.

Though Matt had promised to teach her to ride in a weekend, the lessons had stretched into the second week. Every day for the last ten days they'd worked with Faith.

Amy quickly realized there was much more to riding a horse than putting a saddle on her back and galloping across the countryside. Matt was adamant she knew how to properly care for the horse and tack, as well as how to ride. The lessons had started with a crash course in confirmation, which Amy learned was another name for a horse's physical characteristics.

"You need to know the different parts of the horse," Matt had said. "Trust me, this may be boring, but it'll come in handy as you learn how to handle, groom and tack up."

He'd lost her attention with *trust me.*

Her instinct to trust him once before had saved her life. Now she wondered. If she trusted him again, might she find her life?

But she did trust Faith. That was easy. And for the first time since Garry's betrayal, Amy felt real joy. With Lila feeling better, Amy slipped the cell phone into her pocket and hurried to the barn at sunrise to spend a few minutes with Faith before she started each day with Lila. And in the early evening, when Aunt Lila had settled down with a book or a visiting friend in the living room, Amy practiced the riding techniques Matt had taught her.

Though she was still a novice, she'd mastered the basics of walking, trotting and galloping. Matt praised her for her natural balance and good posture. Once she'd started riding she couldn't get enough, and every free moment she had she found herself in the corral practicing the balancing exercises and school figures Matt had shown her.

"Whoa," Amy said to Faith in a gentle voice as she pressed her lower legs in and increased the feel of her reins, bringing the Morgan to a halt. Together, they gazed at the sinking ball of color. Burnished oranges, reds and yellows spread across the summer sky as if cans of paint had been accidentally overturned. Amy inhaled deeply, enjoying the beauty and majesty of God.

"It's breathtaking, isn't it?" Matt said. She'd been so engrossed with the horse and the sunset she hadn't heard him approach.

"Incredible," she said.

It was funny, she thought, how learning to ride Faith had made her feel more comfortable around Matt. If a horse could trust him, then it didn't seem like such a huge risk for her to trust him. She smiled inwardly at the crazy logic.

"What's so amusing?" Matt asked.

"Nothing. Nothing at all," Amy insisted. And as if to back her up, Faith shook her head.

Petting Faith, Matt said, "Well, I know how tight-lipped you girls can be with your secrets, so I won't even try to pry this one from you. But just to prove what a gentleman I am, I'll lead Faith back to her stall and settle her in for the night."

"Thank you, but Faith and I sort of have our own routine."

Matt raised his eyebrows in a questioning manner. "Okay then. I'll be in the office if you need anything."

Amy nodded, dismounted, then led Faith to her

stall. Though it didn't take long to brush Faith and prepare her for the night, Amy lingered, petting and singing to the horse. Finally, even Faith grew tired and nudged Amy from the stall.

From the far end of the stable Amy heard the soft lull of classical music. Looking down the wide stall-lined aisle, she noticed the light in Matt's office was still on. She would say a quick good-night and then head to the house.

She found Matt staring at a computer screen, rubbing his forehead. As if he sensed her presence, he looked her way and smiled. The weary look on his face instantly dissolved into pleasure.

"I thought you'd have gone back to the house by now," he said, moving a stack of file folders so she could sit.

"I like hanging out here. And your aunt Louise is visiting, so I don't have to hurry back to the house."

"I'm glad Aunt Lila's doing so well," Matt said, as he hit a few buttons on his computer and closed the program he was working on.

"She's made great progress. In fact, I'm really starting to feel useless." When Matt started to interrupt, she raised her hand to stop him. "But don't worry, I'm not going anywhere. Though she's doing great, I don't think she's up to planning a wedding yet."

However, Amy didn't know if she was ready to handle the stress of a second wedding, either. But she'd know by the end of the week.

"The bridesmaids are arriving tomorrow?" Matt asked.

Amy nodded. "All eight of them."

Matt shook his head and laughed. "Even as a kid, I can remember my cousin Tam saying she was going to have the biggest wedding Lexington ever imagined."

"It's certainly going to be grand," Amy said, thinking about how modest her wedding to Garry was supposed to have been.

"You don't approve?" Matt asked.

"It's not that," Amy said. "It's just not my taste. I'd prefer a more intimate ceremony with just a few close friends and family." *And if I ever do plan another wedding, it won't be for a long, long time.*

"Me, too," Matt said.

"I think people spend too much on weddings and honeymoons today. It seems more sensible to put the money toward a down payment on a house. Something that's really going to make a difference in the years to come."

When Matt stared at her with an odd expression, she said, "I know...I'm too practical."

"Not at all. I couldn't agree more. All the lace and flowers and wedding cakes in the world can't make a good marriage. It's the days and years after the honeymoon that really count."

"Or in my case," Amy said, "it's what happens before you say 'I do.'"

But this time, her thoughts didn't linger on Garry. Instead, her thoughts turned to Matt and what a handsome groom he would be. She could imagine his wedding day clearly. He'd wear a black tux with a white rose boutonniere and a smile that would rival the brightness of the stars. And when his bride started down the aisle, his gaze would make her feel as if she were the only woman in the world.

Unintentionally, Amy lifted her head, and when she did, she found herself looking directly into Matt's dark blue eyes. She inhaled swiftly but quietly, amazed by their intensity and longing. And for a split second, Amy felt as if she were the only woman in Matt's world.

Unnerved by the honest emotion in his eyes, Amy panicked. Rising suddenly, she pushed the chair aside, stumbling over her feet as she mumbled a feeble excuse for leaving so abruptly.

Without glancing back, she knew Matt watched from the doorway as she scurried down the stall-lined aisle.

"Good night, Amy," she heard him call.

Chapter Nine

Overcome with embarrassment after her rude departure from Matt's office, Amy avoided Matt and the stables for several days. But in the end, it was Leap of Faith's heartfelt whinnies that lured her back into Matt's territory. Besides, she told herself repeatedly, she was making a mountain out of a molehill. She'd been so consumed with wedding thoughts that she'd probably misread the look in Matt's eyes.

That morning as she walked the short distance from the house to the stable, Amy found her pace quickening and a strange tranquillity descending upon her shoulders as she drew nearer the barns. Until then, she hadn't realized how much she missed the distinctive smells of oats, hay and straw or the rich scent of freshly groomed horses.

As she slipped inside the main doors unnoticed, the clock tower chimed the half hour. For an instant, she thought she'd entered a holy sanctuary. Wide shafts of sunlight streamed in through high windows and crisscrossed the stable floor. The air felt crisp and refreshing as the summer breeze whisked through the open doors at either end of the barn. Deep inside her heart she believed she'd come home. Shaking her head, she chided herself for the silly thought. Living with Lila was only a temporary arrangement. One that would be over at the end of the summer.

Because it seemed like the natural thing to do, she began tending to Faith's daily needs herself. Each morning and evening, she fed and watered the mare, groomed her and mucked out her stall. Matt's stable boy, Billy, didn't seem to mind the extra help. And with each day, Amy found herself doing more and more of Billy's work. It wasn't until the fourth morning that she ran into Matt. Literally.

Singing an old hymn she loved as she carried the heavy bucket of grain, she never heard Matt's boots on the cement floor. It wasn't until she rounded the corner and dumped the oats all over him that she knew he was in the stable. Usually, by this late in the morning, he'd already left for his accounting offices in town.

"I'm sorry," Amy said. Then, seeing the oats piled on Matt's boots, she began to laugh. And when she couldn't stop laughing, Matt joined in with her. Squatting, he scooped up about a quarter of the oats, and then before Amy realized his plan, he poured them over her head.

"Now that's funny," he said.

Using both hands, she batted the oats from her hair

and shoulders. When she reached for the bucket in playful retaliation, Matt grabbed her firmly by the arms and held her at bay. But her playful attack was ended when she began to sneeze.

After a half dozen unstoppable sneezes, she looked at him through errant strands of hair. Though their laughter had faded, Matt still held her by the arms. When she met his gaze, she realized she hadn't been wrong the other night. The light that had illuminated his eyes then had returned, and if he hadn't been holding on to her, her knees would have buckled. For just a second, she thought he was going to pull her closer and kiss her. But then, just as quickly, he released her. As she backed away, she couldn't be certain if he'd really wanted to kiss her or if that had been what she'd wanted.

Matt busied himself with shaking his legs, ridding himself of the last of the clinging oats. Then he helped her, brushing his hands across her arms and back and the top of her head with quick, light strokes.

"I didn't think you'd be here this late," she said, compelled to break the awkward silence between them.

"I'm not going into the office today. There's nothing pressing there, so I thought I'd catch up on some odd jobs around here." That explained why he was wearing jeans and not a tailored suit on a weekday.

"How about you?" There was something about the way he asked the question that told her he'd already formed his own opinion as to her presence.

"It's getting a little crazy in the house. I thought some fresh air would do me good."

"The bridesmaids have arrived," Matt said with a wicked grin.

"All eight of them." Amy was all for tradition, but even so, eight excited women plus a bride made Aunt Lila's spacious home seem tiny and cramped. "It's unreal."

Glancing toward the house, Amy noted that except for the extra cars in the driveway, all appeared normal from this distance. But looks were deceiving. Inside, it was like a college reunion at a sorority dorm. And though she'd instantly liked all of Tam's bridesmaids, she couldn't wait to escape to the serenity of the stables and hills. As soon as Lila's sister had arrived to help, Amy had taken the opportunity to disappear.

"How long before you have to be back?" Matt asked, nodding toward the house.

"A couple of hours at the most," Amy said, checking her watch. She'd already been gone a half hour. But she had the cell phone with her, so she wasn't out of touch. Lila and Louise had already decided to have lunch catered. There wasn't anything pressing for Amy to do.

"Let's squeeze in a ride."

Amy nodded, thinking nothing would please her more.

After saddling Faith, she took a minute to call Lila and make her aware of her plans.

"Now, you take all the time you need, dear. I'm just fine. Louise is with me, and all the girls, of course. Plans are running smoothly. After lunch, I'll take a nice long nap.''

Amy shook her head, because she knew better. ''With all the excitement, I don't want you to forget to take your medicine.''

''Louise will help me keep an eye on the time. Don't give me another thought. Just go and have a good time.''

''I'll check in with you soon,'' Amy promised. After closing the flip phone, she stuffed it into her shirt pocket.

''All set?'' Matt asked. He led a large chestnut stallion named Winner across the corral and opened the gate.

''I'm ready. I need to be back by noon, though,'' she said, purposely ignoring Lila's instructions.

With Matt in the lead, they rode across the meadow and deep into the woods, following a narrow path beside the meandering stream. Sunlight, filtered by outstretched leaves and branches on towering oaks and maples, fell to the ground in kaleidoscope fashion. Unseen finches, orioles and chickadees chirped, while gray squirrels raced alongside in the underbrush.

Finally, the thick trees gave way to a meadow carpeted with tall grasses and a pond surrounded by wildflowers. On the bank, a lone willow tree offered shade, a place to tie the horses as well as a low branch to sit on.

From a saddle pack, Matt pulled thermoses of iced tea and granola bars.

"I didn't even think about packing a snack," Amy said, enjoying the refreshment as she watched dragonflies flit across the smooth water.

"You stay around Aunt Lila long enough, and her form of hospitality will become second nature."

"I've already picked up a few tips," Amy said. "Like how to stretch a dinner for four to feed six. How to organize a house when you're expecting eight female guests. Not to mention that it's almost a sin if you don't have a plate of cookies or a pitcher of iced tea ready to serve anytime guests drop by. Which, with your family, is often."

"She's the best," Matt said.

Taking the tiny opening Matt had given her, Amy said, "We talked the other day about how well Aunt Lila is doing. At her last appointment, her doctor said her recovery is ahead of schedule. And though I'm planning to live with her for a while longer, I thought you should know she isn't going to need me for the entire summer. I'm sure she's going to want to be on her own soon, and I know it's important to her to prove she doesn't have to rely on anyone."

Matt's gaze followed the distant rise and fall of the surrounding hills. When he turned back to Amy, he smiled as if he had a plan in mind. "I think Aunt Lila loves having you live with her. I'd be really surprised if she asks you to leave before the summer is up."

Amy shook her head. "Of course, she's not going to ask me to leave. She's too softhearted. All along, she's believed I needed her more than she's needed me."

"Well, that was the only way we could get her to accept help. And she did need help when you first moved in." Matt finished his iced tea and screwed the top of his thermos on tight. "And I'm very grateful for the compassionate care you've given her."

Amy nonchalantly waved her hand. "I didn't do anything special. Your aunt is easy to love." *And so are you.* The thought came from out of nowhere and nearly scared Amy to death.

But Garry had been easy to love, too, and look what had happened, she quickly reminded herself.

Matt waited until Amy met his gaze before he spoke. "Are you trying to tell me *you* want to leave? Soon?"

Amy swallowed, then bit her lip. No, she didn't want to leave. But if she didn't go soon, she was afraid she might do something she would regret. One look into Matt's caring eyes, and she knew her fears were justified.

"I think I should move out in a week or two."

"And where would you go? Do you have a new job and apartment located?" The way he fired the questions one after the other reminded her of her father.

"No, but in my free time, I'm starting to look." It was only in the last two weeks that she'd been able to focus on her future. And she owed her renewed hope to Lila and their morning prayer walks. Amazingly, it was during this silent time with God that she felt her hurting heart heal a little more each day. During this time, she began to see the bigger picture. That if it hadn't been for the pain Garry had inflicted, she'd never have left Ohio in desperation and ended up in Matt's arms.

She owed him so much. Because of his courage and kindness, she'd spent the last few weeks living with a wise woman of faith on this Kentucky horse farm. She couldn't help but believe God had known exactly what she'd needed when she'd left Ohio in her rearview mirror.

"Any good prospects?" Matt asked. Shifting his weight to straddle the low willow branch, he faced her directly, his concern seemingly genuine.

"Not really," Amy said. Embarrassed, she looked away. "All my friends back home decided upon college and career paths before they'd graduated from high school. But it's never been that easy for me. Right out of high school I got a good job in a local bank where I thought I had a future. But I never really enjoyed the work. I'm interested in a lot of things, but I've never been excited enough about any one thing to devote myself to it."

Except maybe since she moved to this farm. Discovering how much she loved working in Lila's herb garden on warm summer afternoons had been a pleasant surprise. And she enjoyed working with the horses, too. While the work was demanding, it left her with a satisfaction she hadn't felt in a long time. If ever. But she didn't see either as a career.

"It seems like the more uncertain you are of yourself, the more pressure you feel. And the more pressure you feel, the harder it is to make a decision. At least, that's been my experience," Matt said. Reaching down, he plucked a thick strand of tall grass and idly rolled the green blade between his fingers. His eyes narrowed and his head bobbed as if he had a solution to her problems. "Maybe you're looking at this decision from the wrong angle."

"How's that?" Amy asked, receptive to his opinion.

"Maybe you're trying to make a lifelong decision, and that's too scary. Most of us don't know what we're going to be doing six months from now, let alone twenty years down the road."

"You could be onto something." The thought of dedicating herself to a field for the rest of her life was daunting.

"I like to think in five-year increments," Matt said.

Amy smiled. "Somehow, I think the accountant in you is shining through."

Matt blushed slightly, and when he did Amy was suddenly aware of how handsome he looked in the willow shade. Anchoring a strand of windblown hair behind her ear, she tried to concentrate on what he said and not on how perfectly his soft, tender lips formed each word.

"Seriously, I like to break things into manageable units of time and work. Then the project doesn't seem so overwhelming."

Amy nodded. While this wasn't new information, she'd never thought of if it in relation to her career choices.

"For instance, think about what job you'd like to

do for the next five years. And then ask yourself what you need to do in order to get that job. Do you need a college degree or to pass a state exam? Do you need a certain type of work experience? Then you break your plan down to what you need to do today.''

"This works for you, doesn't it?" Before he nodded, she could tell by the tilt of his head and the steady gleam in his eyes that this was the way he lived his life. He decided what he wanted and he went after it. She envied him that. Knowing what you wanted was something to be treasured.

"I'd be happy to ask around and see if any of my clients have a job opening," Matt said. "That is, if you want my help. I'd understand—"

"Oh, no," Amy said. "I appreciate your help more than you know."

"Well, we'll put out a Wynn family memo then. One of us ought to be able to come up with a job that's perfect for you."

Touching him lightly on the wrist, she said, "Thank you. You've done so much for me."

"Not really. Besides, someday when you're on your feet, you'll help someone else."

"That's a wonderful way to see the world," she said. "One big circle. What you give eventually comes back to you."

Matt sighed, and his smile suddenly didn't seem so steady. "That's true. But things don't always come back as soon as you'd like. And often not in the way you'd like."

Intrigued, Amy leaned closer, needing to see as

deeply into his eyes as he'd allow her to. "What is it that you want?"

As soon as she asked the question, she remembered their talk on the hilltop and how he'd shared his dreams about marriage and children. Until this moment, she hadn't realized how desperately he wanted those dreams to have come true yesterday.

Matt gazed into the distance, and for a moment, she didn't think he was going to answer her.

"I'd really like to know," she said softly.

When he turned to her, his eyes sagged with heaviness. "I've planned my life so carefully. I've built a dependable accounting business. I own a modest house and I have a growing savings account. I adore my nieces and nephews and I belong to a wonderful church." When he spoke there was an objectivity that didn't leave room for self-pity.

"You have a pretty good life," she said.

"I have a full life, but it's also a lonely life," Matt said. "I'm tired of coming home at the end of the day to an empty house, to solitary dreams."

Amy inhaled deeply, attuned to his vulnerability. And she felt they'd come full circle, too, with him once again seeking her reassurance that love did come to those who sought happy endings. But she still couldn't tell him that. It wouldn't be honest. It certainly hadn't been her experience.

Feeling bold, she offered some advice. "I think you need to quit pining for what you don't have and concentrate on what you do have. You have a wonderful life, Matthew Wynn, and when God's good and ready He'll bring the perfect woman into your life."

"Is that so?" Matt asked, a tiny bit of hope sparking in his blue eyes.

"That's so," Amy said. "But then what do I know about God's plans?"

"Oh, I think—"

She never did hear what he thought because her cellular telephone rang, and she suddenly realized it was way past lunchtime.

"Just checking in," Lila said. "I've had my lunch and medicine, and I'm headed upstairs for a nap. So, enjoy the rest of the afternoon."

Amy said goodbye to Lila and then said to Matt, "I need to get back. Lila needs me."

On the ride home, as Amy stared at the strong contour of Matt's back and the protective curve of his long arms, she recalled how easy it had been to trust him in the dark convenience store closet. It was the connection they'd forged there, grounded in the basic need for survival, that made it easy for them to reveal their most vulnerable secrets. It was the only thing that made sense, she thought.

For the rest of the afternoon, Matt couldn't think of anything except Amy's plans to leave his aunt's farm. Maybe even Kentucky. Soon. Though he couldn't pinpoint the exact reason, his gut reaction convinced him she'd be making a huge mistake, and he had to stop her. She wasn't back on her feet yet. And he'd promised God he'd help Amy get her life on track. Before she moved out, she needed to secure a dependable job and save a few weeks' wages. Somehow, he had to convince her she was welcome to stay at the farm as long as necessary.

It wasn't until after sunset that Matt had a chance to talk to Aunt Lila alone.

"Amy's talking about moving out," he said. "She doesn't feel like she's needed here."

Looking directly at him, Aunt Lila said, "I'm not the one who needs her."

Matt shook his head at Lila's directness. He shouldn't have been surprised by her assessment of the situation, but she was wrong. He and Amy were only friends, albeit good friends. He'd never dared to open the door to his heart with anyone as wide as he had with her today under the willow tree. But then he didn't expect Aunt Lila to understand the true nature of their relationship. They'd survived a terrible ordeal together and formed a lasting bond. After what they'd been through, it was only natural he cared about Amy.

"Amy needs us," he insisted. "She's making some important decisions, and I'd hate to see her rush out of here because she feels like she's overstayed her welcome.

"Then give her something to do. Make her feel needed." Kissing Matt on the cheek, she added, "I know you'll think of something. It's past my bedtime."

Matt lingered at the bottom of the steps, mulling his aunt's advice. *Give her something to do.* But what? His accounting firm was small, and she'd know instantly if he created a place for her there. No, she wouldn't agree to that.

When eight women with blue mud on their faces and sponge wedges separating their freshly painted toenails rushed past him and up the stairway, Matt felt like he'd just encountered a whirlwind. Eager to escape the joyous turmoil, he sought quiet relief in the stables. In the past, he'd done some of his best thinking among the horses.

And apparently, so did Amy.

He stopped when he saw her standing next to Leap of Faith's stall. He couldn't hear what she said to the black Morgan, but judging by the serious line of her profile, it was a very important conversation.

In a flash, the idea struck him.

He knew exactly what Amy needed.

When Amy looked Leap of Faith in the eyes, she felt confident the horse understood her woes.

"I've never had a friend like you," she confided. "You always listen. You never interrupt. And best of all, you always take my side." Amy petted the mare, who offered a sympathetic whinny in response. "But don't worry. I'm sure Aunt Lila and Matt will allow me visiting rights once I've moved out. I can't imagine living without you."

Amy leaned over the waist-high gate and kissed Faith on the neck. "Get some rest, girl," she said.

For the past few hours, Amy had thought of nothing but leaving the farm. But where would she go? So far there'd been nothing in the classified ads that had captured her interest. She'd read a half dozen books on selecting and changing careers but still had no direction. She did learn a few good tips and had made a list of things to do. By the end of the week, she intended to stop by the university to pick up their fall catalogue and meet with a career counselor. Because she was fairly certain she would go back to school, she needed a good paying job with flexible hours to support her while she earned her degree.

But if she was going to spend all this time and energy going back to school, then she'd better decide what she wanted to study. Amy sighed. The daily prayer walk wasn't cutting it. It looked like she might have to sign up for a marathon.

When Amy came downstairs the next morning, it was to a quiet household. Lila was already up and dressed and had a cup of green tea poured for her.

"I feel like getting out of the house," Lila announced. "Tam's got her wedding under complete control. She inherited the organizational gene from me," Lila said, then winked. "Besides, I need a break from all this hoopla."

"What did you have in mind?" Amy asked, thinking Lila might like to hike to the top of Matt's hilltop or ride the horses out to the pond and enjoy a picnic lunch.

"Let's explore Shakertown," she suggested.

"That sounds like a grand idea." With only three days until Rob and Tam's wedding, Amy was eager for a break from bridal hairdos, satin shoes and the sappy love songs the bridesmaids played nonstop.

Lila clapped her hands. "Oh, I was hoping you'd say yes. I know Matt would hit the roof if I drove down by myself. He is too protective."

"He loves you dearly," Amy said, though it wasn't necessary. Lila knew she was loved.

"And I love you, too, dear," Lila added, as she kissed Amy on the cheek. "From the day you moved in, you've been like one of the family."

Stunned by the warm affection, Amy stuttered, "I—I love you, too."

"Well, then it's settled. I won't hear anymore nonsense about you moving out until the end of the summer."

Now Amy understood. Matt had told Lila about her plans. Though it angered her that he'd broken her confidence, she was glad in a way. It reminded her he couldn't be trusted.

Amy and Lila left the house and were traveling down Harrodsburg Road before the sleeping bridesmaids even thought about opening their eyes. Within minutes, the scenic countryside relaxed Amy as they wound through wooded areas and past pristine farms. Once in Shakertown, Aunt Lila insisted they start with a boat ride on the Kentucky River aboard the *Dixie Belle*. Surrounded by majestic palisades, Amy lost her breath as she absorbed nature's timeless beauty. At lunchtime, they ate in the authentic Shaker dining room, savoring the best hot brown sandwich and lemon chess pie she'd ever tasted.

As they leisurely strolled through the village buildings—the meetinghouse, the trustee's office, the water house, the post office and the cooper's shop—it was easy for Amy to imagine a simpler life.

"The Shakers were an innovative and industrious group of people," Lila said on the drive home. "The thing I've always admired most about them is how they see everything they do—from the wash to growing crops to carpentry to assisting others—as a form of worship and praise."

"That made an impression on me, too," Amy said, suddenly realizing Lila's real motive behind this little excursion.

"What you do isn't as important as how you do it," Lila continued. "When you consider everything you do as a way of praising God, then even the smallest, most insignificant tasks take on greater meaning."

Glancing at Lila, Amy said, "What would I ever do without you?"

The warmth in Lila's blue eyes touched Amy. "You won't have to worry about that, dear, for a long, long time."

Somewhere along the way, Lila had become like a second mother to Amy. As they whizzed down the highway, she reflected on how much her life had changed just because she'd been trapped in a convenience store during a robbery. Some would have said she'd been in the wrong place at the wrong time. But with each day Amy spent at the Wynn farm, it became more clear that she'd been exactly where God had wanted her to be. Obviously, He'd felt the need to do something drastic in order to get her attention. And now He had it. With every morning she spent walking in respectful meditation and prayer, she grew closer to God. It wasn't something she could quantify or prove, but it was an awareness that ran through her heart. The bitterness, the anger and the hurt inflicted by Garry were still there, but they were constantly crowded and jostled by the new joy and wisdom growing within her.

Gripping the steering wheel as she rounded a sharp curve, she said, "Ever since I left Ohio, I've felt this urgency to decide what I was going to do for the rest of my life. I've felt if I didn't do something now, time would slip away, and all of a sudden I'd be thirty or forty and still thinking about going back to school."

"The years do have a way of slipping by us," Lila agreed. "Urgency is God's way of nudging you into a new phase of your life. But make sure you don't make a decision just to make a decision."

Amy nodded. Until they'd visited Shakertown she'd been tempted to do just that. But the afternoon spent wandering through a village of the past had given her new perspective. She'd been so focused on selecting a career she judged worthwhile that she'd done nothing more than spin around in a frustrated circle. Now her vision had been expanded. Any work God called her into, no matter how menial, was important. The key was her attitude.

"I've got a good feeling," she said. "I don't want to sound cocky, but by the end of summer, I think I'm going to have a new job and a new home."

Lila nodded in agreement. "There's no doubt about

it. In fact, I think God has something very special in store for you.''

The sparkle in Lila's eyes drew a smile from Amy. She couldn't help but wonder what secret God had just whispered in the elder woman's ear.

Chapter Ten

When Matt realized neither Amy nor his aunt was at home, he didn't worry. But as the morning sun crossed into the afternoon sky, he began to wonder where they could be. He'd trusted Amy to take care of his aunt, and up to this point she had. However, Lila certainly wasn't up to a long, exhausting outing. What could Amy have been thinking?

Soon his uneasiness turned to dread. Was it possible they'd been in an accident or that Aunt Lila had had an episode and Amy had taken her to the hospital? No, that wasn't probable. If anything had happened, Amy or the police would have contacted him by now.

Finally, he decided to end the speculation and call Amy on her cellular telephone. When Aunt Lila answered, sounding cheerful and energetic, he released a long sigh.

"We're almost home," she said. "We'll be there in ten minutes."

"It sounds like you've had an enjoyable day," he said, giving her the chance to explain their whereabouts.

"We went to Shakertown," Aunt Lila said. "And it was a lovely day."

"That's great," he said, suddenly feeling foolish for calling. He should have known Amy would never harm his aunt. In fact, it pleased him to see how close the two women had grown. His God-given instinct had been right. Amy belonged on this horse farm for the summer.

And maybe longer. The unexpected thought bubbled up from deep within. As long as Aunt Lila was happy, he reasoned, Amy could stay as long as she pleased. And he knew the rest of his family would agree.

Not wanting Amy or Lila to know worry had prompted his call he said, "Would you tell Amy I'd like to talk to her when she gets back? Tell her I'll be working in the stable."

He waited while Lila relayed his message. "She'll see you in a few minutes."

"Great." Matt ended the call. He hadn't planned to spring his plan on Amy until after Rob and Tam's wedding, but today seemed as good a time as ever. And he knew exactly where to ask her.

As he'd expected, as soon as Amy walked Aunt Lila to the house, she went directly to see Faith. From a safe distance, he watched her stroke the horse's neck, murmuring soft caring words that delighted Faith.

Even from this distance, he could detect a subtle change in the way Amy held her head and shoulders as well as the arch of her back. With each day she grew more confident and self-assured, which meant it was only a matter of time before she felt the need to leave.

Approaching quietly, he didn't speak until he was at her side.

"Hello," he said.

Amy jumped, and Faith's ears perked up with agitation. "Matt's rule of horsemanship," Amy quoted without looking at him, "never sneak up behind a horse. Approach quietly and confidently, with no sudden movements." She paused, then turned to point a finger at him. "I believe that's on page seven of the Wynn handbook."

Matt placed his hands on her shoulders and rotated her slightly toward him. He shook her gently. "You think you're cute, don't you?"

With the brief touch, a memory from the convenience store surged through his body. For a split second, he wanted to pull her into his arms, as he had in the closet, to see if she still felt like a perfect fit. Instead, he abruptly dropped his hands to his sides.

Glancing over her shoulder, Amy looked at Faith. "The horse thinks I'm cute."

"Her opinion is prejudiced."

"And you're claiming to be objective?" Amy asked.

Though it was said in jest, Matt realized any opinions he had concerning Amy were far from objective. He didn't know when it had happened, but at some point he'd gone from seeing her as someone he felt obligated to help to seeing her as a woman with great potential that he wanted to see happy and successful.

"Objective's my middle name," he said, unwilling to reveal his true feelings.

"Okay, Mr. Objective, what was it you wanted to talk to me about? I haven't got all day." Though Amy looked at him without meeting his gaze, he detected a glimmer of curiosity.

"I have a problem, and I thought you might be able to help me out." When she stared at him with her eyes slightly narrowed he knew she'd see through his offer, but he couldn't back down now. And what did he have to lose? The worst she could do was say no and leave the farm.

An odd sensation jolted his heart. Even if she moved out, they'd still remain friends. They'd still see each other from time to time. So why did the thought of her leaving the farm trouble him so? It was the connection from the robbery, he convinced himself. Though he'd been certain it would wear thin with time, it hadn't. And he had to believe that he and Amy would always be connected in this strange sort of way. It was as if God had appointed him her unofficial guardian angel.

"Exactly what is it I can do for you?" Amy asked, crossing her arms over her chest in case she needed protection.

Matt pressed his lips together, using his tongue to moisten them. His mouth had suddenly gone dry as he realized how much he wanted her to say yes.

"Billy's been grounded again," Matt began. "So I'm without help in the stable."

He saw the light dawn in her eyes, and he sent a special thank-you heavenward.

"And you want me to help?" Amy asked, her words edged in disbelief.

"You're already doing half of Billy's work anyway."

"I didn't know you knew," she said, dipping her head with shyness. "I hope I didn't get him in trouble."

Matt shook his head. "So...will you help me out?"

Amy's gaze drifted around the stable as she quietly considered the pros and cons. When she frowned, he feared she was leaning toward no. Then Faith, insistent on making her opinion known, nudged Amy at the back of her waist. Amy instantly turned and hugged the horse.

With her face pressed against Faith's black mane, she said, "Yes, I'll help."

She spoke so low he wasn't certain she'd really agreed. Maybe he'd merely heard what he'd wanted her to say.

When she turned to face him, he ignored the doubt in her eyes. "Thanks. You're a lifesaver."

Amy nodded. "And you can do me a favor, too."

"Anything," he said.

"I'd appreciate it if you didn't discuss my personal

business with Aunt Lila. If I want to confide in her, I will."

At first, he wasn't certain about what she referred to. Then he realized Aunt Lila must have spoken to Amy about her plans to move on. "I'm sorry," he said. "I didn't mean to say anything I shouldn't have. It just sort of came up. I was talking to Aunt Lila about her health and how she was doing."

Amy sighed. "No harm done. It's just important to me that I make my own decisions. That's one of the reasons I left home. I wanted to live my life, not the life my parents thought was best for me."

"Again, I'm sorry about—"

Amy cocked her head. "No harm done. I'm probably being overly sensitive, anyway."

As if Faith had followed the entire conversation, she whinnied with her head high in the air. Matt and Amy looked at each other and laughed. Without thinking, Matt reached out and touched Amy's cheek with his fingertips. The warmth and softness amazed him and made him want to draw her close enough to kiss her.

For a second, he thought she was going to cover his hand with hers. Then she turned away and hurried down the stall-lined aisle. "I assume the job starts immediately," she called when she reached a safe distance.

"No time like the present," Matt said.

"And the pay and benefits are negotiable?"

"You've got me in a bind," he said. And it was

true. Just when he thought he knew how he felt about her, everything flip-flopped.

Amy rounded the corner and slipped into the first empty stall she found. Sinking to her heels in the corner, she leaned against the wooden wall, her forehead against her knees, her hands locked behind her head.

What was she thinking?

Who was that woman who'd wanted to touch Matt's hand? Who was the woman who'd arched forward, praying he wanted to kiss her as badly as she wanted him to kiss her?

More confused than ever, Amy pleaded with God to help her make sense of her emotions. Why did she tell Matt she'd work in the stables when she knew it was time to move on?

She couldn't blame it on Leap of Faith, though the horse's perfectly timed nudge had swayed her to say yes. She couldn't live with Lila forever because she'd fallen in love with a horse.

Was it possible? Was she falling in love with Matt? No. She shook her head.

She knew without a doubt that wasn't true. Because without trust there could be no love. And her heart still wouldn't let her trust a man.

Oh, God, what is happening to me?

And as if God heard her, she felt Him reach down and rip open the secret part of her heart that she'd thought she'd been able to hide even from Him. Within seconds, all the ugly bitterness, resentfulness and humiliation she'd tucked away washed over her. The emotions were so strong, she could almost feel them slide down her body.

Discouraged, Amy began to sob. She thought she'd made real progress since moving to Kentucky. She thought her heart had begun to heal. How could she have deceived herself so? She was just as angry at Garry as the day she'd seen him kissing another woman.

Oh, God, what do I have to do to let go of this hurt? Where am I ever going to find the strength to honestly forgive Garry?

Amy didn't know how long she sat in the corner of the straw-covered stall, but when the clock tower chimed the hour, she knew she'd better finish the chores she promised Matt she'd handle.

Though her heart was heavy and troubled, she recalled what she'd just learned at Shakertown, and she carried every bucket of grain and aired the bedding in each stall with a prayerful attitude. And when she was finished, she was amazed at how peaceful she felt. While her problems were still with her, so was God.

Amy welcomed the distraction of working in the stables. She quickly fell in love with all the horses Matt boarded and enjoyed chatting with their owners when they came to ride.

With Rob and Tam's wedding only a day away and the house suspended in a joyous uproar, Amy craved the privacy and solitude the stables offered more than ever. Keeping the cell phone in her pocket, she could attend to Lila's needs and still spend a majority of her day either in the herb garden or with the horses. Her growing passion for both gardening and riding astounded her, because until she'd moved to Lexington she'd never attempted either.

After packing a quick lunch, she hiked to the top of Matt's hilltop in record time. That was another benefit of living on the Wynn farm. She was in the best shape she'd ever been in. Her arms and legs had grown strong and agile, and she tired less easily. As she followed the path up the hill, her thoughts drifted to when Matt had talked about how his grandfather and father walked life out one step at a time. That's what she was doing, too.

Alone on the hilltop, she stretched her hands above her head and sang out the Westminster chime melody. She was so glad Lila had told her the family story about the clock tower. For each time the chimes rang, she was reminded that God was with her. She'd been naive to believe her heart would heal with a simple prayer or the reading of a scripture. She had to work through her feelings, and that took time. It might be weeks or months before the wounds truly healed. She needed to be patient, though patience was something she hadn't had much of lately.

Avoiding the high boulder where she'd shared an intimate conversation with Matt, she selected a small log to sit on while she ate her lunch and enjoyed the inspiring view.

She unwrapped her sandwich and was about to take the first bite when the telephone rang.

"Amy, it's Tam, and we've got an emergency. Where are you?"

"I'm on the hilltop. I'll be there in a few minutes."

Amy grabbed her lunch bag and ran.

Dear God, please let Lila be okay.

The thought of anything happening to the dear woman shook her to the core.

She arrived at the house winded and red in the face. Charging into the living room, she stopped abruptly when she found Lila, Tam and seven bridesmaids. Lila quietly sat in a tapestry wing chair, while Tam and her bridesmaids paced around the room.

Amy looked from Lila to Tam, puzzled that everyone appeared to be healthy. "What's wrong?" she asked.

"You won't believe this," Tam said, grabbing Amy's hand, "but Brittany, my maid of honor, went for a moonlight horse ride last night. She fell and broke her leg. She's in traction. She won't be able to stand up with me, let alone attend the wedding."

"I'm so sorry," Amy said. "But I'm glad she's okay."

"This is terrible." Tam dropped down on the couch and threw her arm over her eyes.

Amy glanced at Lila, who shrugged her shoulders as if to indicate this was a delicate situation.

"It looks like we need your help," Lila said.

Hadn't Matt said the same thing to her just a few days ago? *Would you help me out?* And she knew that regardless of what Lila asked her, she'd say yes, just as she'd said yes to Matt. They'd both done so much for her, she couldn't let them down.

"What do you need me to do?" she asked, thinking they'd want her to sit with the injured bridesmaid or run last-minute errands.

With doe eyes, Tam said, "I want you to take Brittany's place. It would mean so much to Rob and me."

"Me? Your maid of honor? Surely, one of the other bridesmaids would love to take Brittany's place," Amy insisted.

"They would," Tam agreed. "But the maid of honor's dress is a different style from the rest, and it doesn't fit anyone else. They've all tried it on. If it wasn't too long, it was too short. If it fit at the waist, it was too big across the shoulders. And the seamstress who made the dress is out of town, and I wouldn't dare let anyone else make the alterations. So please, will you try the dress on? Aunt Lila thought you'd be the perfect size."

"But I'm not family," she said. "I'm sure you'd love to have one of your cousins—"

"But you are family to us," Tam insisted. "Anyone that takes as good care of Aunt Lila as you have is a Wynn at heart. And that's what counts."

Seeing she wasn't going to be able to argue her way out of this, Amy closed her eyes briefly. If she tried the dress on and it fit, she'd have no choice but to say yes. Not only would she be attending the wedding, she'd be walking down the aisle.

Oh, God, how can I survive that? She hadn't even

been able to stay in the sanctuary during Dave and Susy's ceremony.

Taking a deep breath, she agreed to try the dress on, though silently she prayed it wouldn't fit.

With a hopeful smile, Tam handed her the peach organza dress. Then in a quivering voice she said, "When everything seemed to be going smoothly, I knew it was too good to be true."

Amy's heart softened just a bit, and she smiled at Tam. The bride-to-be who'd seemed only yesterday to be in complete control was crumbling under the stress.

"I'll give it a try," Amy promised, as she slipped into her bedroom and shut the door. As an afterthought, she called, "I'd better take a shower first. I've been working with the horses all morning, and I wouldn't want to soil the fabric."

Amy deliberately took her time in the shower, letting the water splash over her soapy skin. From the hallway she could hear Tam pacing, and every few minutes the nervous bride would call, "Does it fit?"

Finally, Amy emerged from the shower, towel dried and, inhaling deeply, picked up the dress and stepped into the sheer silk organza. The peachy color complemented her newly tanned skin. Pushing her arms through the sleeve holes, she knew before buttoning the dress that it was going to be a perfect fit.

Looking at herself in the mirror, she faced her greatest fear. Did she tell Tam yes, or did she take the cowardly way out?

Deep within, she knew the answer. This was what

Matt's grandfather had meant when he'd said you had to walk out life one step at a time. If she ever wanted her heart to heal and to move on with her life, she had to walk down that aisle tomorrow.

Opening the door a crack, Amy let Tam in. "I couldn't button it," she said.

With trembling fingers, Tam fastened the long row of fabric-covered buttons. When she finished, she twirled Amy around twice to be certain of what she saw. But instead of a triumphant smile, Tam burst into tears.

Amy grasped both the bride-to-be's hands and said, "It's going to be okay."

Though she looked into Tam's eyes, it was to her heart that she made the promise.

Amy waited in the dressing room in the church basement with seven bridesmaids and the flower girl. Though the dress draped her slim body as if it had been made for her, she didn't feel comfortable in the peach organza. With as many bridesmaids as Tam had, she still didn't see why one of them couldn't have stepped into Brittany's place. But this was Tam's wedding, and Tam had always dreamed it would be a certain way.

When Amy's thoughts drifted to the time when she'd been planning her wedding to Garry, she stopped them cold. She wasn't going to focus on what could have been. She was going to think about what could be.

"We're almost ready to start," Aunt Lila said.

"I'm going to take my seat. You all know what to do." Walking over to Tam, she clasped the bride's hands, kissed her on the cheek and said, "May God richly bless you and Rob."

Then at the doorway she paused. "Remember, girls, don't walk too fast."

"We'll be fine," someone called.

Amy followed the other bridesmaids to the back of the church, as they'd done at rehearsal the night before. In the foyer, Tam and her father waited while the bridal party started down the aisle.

When it was Amy's turn, she thought her knees would buckle. *Please, God,* she prayed. *Help me take this step.* And though she'd taken millions of steps in her life, she sensed that this was one of the most important. If she could take this step, she knew she could defeat any fear that would come her way in the future.

To the beat of the music, Amy started down the aisle, walking slowly with even steps as Aunt Lila had instructed. Though the church was full of family and friends, the smiling faces blurred into one creamy texture. Amy looked neither left nor right, but kept her eyes focused on the altar ahead.

It wasn't until she passed the front pew that she saw Matt. For a second their eyes connected, and he smiled at her with an intensity that bolstered her strength and confidence. She stumbled for just a second then veered left and took her proper place.

But she couldn't keep her gaze off Matt.

What was he doing here?

Then it hit her. He was the best man. As soon as Rob and Tam said "I do" and kissed, Amy had to walk down the aisle on Matt's arm.

While everyone else admired the bride who slowly floated down the white carpet, Amy glanced at Matt. This time, when their eyes met, she was too mesmerized to look away.

In all the time she'd dated Garry, he'd never looked at her with such respect and reverence. He'd never looked at her as if he thought she could conquer the world.

At the time, she'd thought Garry had loved her, but now she knew differently. She and Garry hadn't known the first thing about real love and commitment. And if she were honest, there had been signs along the way that Garry hadn't been ready to settle down and get married.

Even still, knowing this didn't make his betrayal hurt any less. It just reminded her of how poor her judgment had been. And was it any better now? Had she really changed and grown in these last few weeks?

What she saw in Matt's eyes scared her. She felt as if he'd invited her into his soul, and surprisingly, she wanted to go. She wanted to know his deepest fears and biggest dreams. She wanted to share his joys and his troubles.

Her feelings toward Matt were changing. What had started out as a survivor connection in a closet had grown into a deeper friendship. Though it was hard to admit, she was starting to trust this man.

Then doubt crept in, and Amy looked away. Before she could trust Matt, she had to be able to trust herself and her judgment. Wasn't it possible she was misreading this situation, just as she'd misread Garry's love? Matt cared about her as a friend; he'd never tried to hide that. He was a kindhearted man, and when he'd sensed her life was in turmoil he'd reached out a helping hand. Matt had never given her any indication he was interested in anything more.

Biting her bottom lip, Amy fought back the tears. Concentrating on each breath, she dug deep and found a strength that could only have come from God.

Someday, I'll be able to fall in love, she prayed. *Someday, it'll be my wedding day.*

Before she could stop herself, her gaze returned to Matt. As if he could read her mind, he slowly nodded and smiled.

The minister said, "I now pronounce you man and wife. You may kiss the bride."

As Amy watched Rob and Tam seal their love, in her heart she dreamed it was her and Matt celebrating love with a kiss.

Chapter Eleven

When Matt offered Amy his arm, it wasn't as difficult to accept as she'd feared. Still, she held her breath as they followed the bride and groom down the aisle, exhaling only after they'd reached the church foyer and formed the receiving line. For once, she was grateful for the abundance of Wynns, because the constant stream of family prevented her and Matt from exchanging a single private word.

As she shook hands, hugged and exchanged pleasantries with those passing by, she was surprised at how many relatives she'd gotten to know in the last few weeks. With confidence, she called his parents, all the aunts and uncles, as well as the cousins and their spouses by name. It was only the youngest generation that she couldn't keep straight. But given time…

As soon as the last hand was shaken, the wedding party quickly assembled in the sanctuary to take group photographs. Amy stood next to Matt. The photographer instructed him to place his hand on Amy's shoulder. For a brief moment, just as she felt his touch, his woodsy scent lured her back to the time she'd spent in his arms in the closet. The memory brought a smile to her lips, and without thinking she glanced at Matt as the camera flashed.

Swallowing hard, she inwardly cringed, knowing how sappy she was going to look in that photograph. No doubt, she'd be mistakenly identified as a lovesick puppy. Why did the slightest scent of Matt recall that dark hour? Why did those memories still feel as real as yesterday?

Thankfully, Amy didn't have time to ponder those questions as the photographer called instructions for the next pose, asking everyone to please take their positions quickly. Later, as they were ushered into cars for the ride to a historic mansion for the reception, Amy managed to take the last seat in a limousine without Matt. If at all possible, without being rude, she intended to avoid him at the reception.

As soon as the Mansion at Griffin Gate came into view, she understood exactly why the bride had chosen this two-story antebellum home for her reception. Surrounded by majestic blue ash, chinquapin oak and Kentucky coffee trees on a grassy knoll, the nearly one-hundred-and-fifty-year-old mansion conjured up fairytale dreams.

Once inside, she felt like she'd stepped back in time. Furnished with rare antiques, original artwork and sparkling crystal chandeliers, the nineteenth century estate recreated a grand past. Because it had once been a home, it was easy to wander through the series of connecting rooms, visiting with family and friends, always careful to remain one step ahead of Matt.

Throughout dinner, the cutting of the cake and even the first dance, Amy's efforts were rewarded. It wasn't until the family had gathered outside to watch the Fourth of July fireworks that she accidentally let her guard down. At the first hint of his richly scented cologne, she knew Matt stood behind her.

Moving to within inches of her back, he whispered, "Only Tam would think the Fourth of July fireworks were just for her."

Squeezing her eyes shut, she tried to convince herself that the warm rush of his breath on her neck didn't please her. She tried to tell herself that she didn't feel safer, more peaceful, just because he was near enough to wrap his arms around her.

"I envy her confidence," Amy said, turning her thoughts to the happy bride.

"You know she wasn't always like that."

"She wasn't?" Amy said with disbelief.

"I remember a skinny little kid who was too shy to raise her hand in Sunday school."

"What happened?"

"I don't know for sure. Maybe it was Aunt Lila's pep talks. Maybe she just grew up. Or maybe she fell in love with the right man."

Intrigued by Matt's observations, Amy studied Tam. Was it possible that falling in love with the right man could change your life? Could love bring out the best in a person in a way nothing or no one else could?

The instant Matt leaned closer, Amy knew he was going to place his hands on her shoulders. While his grip was firm, it wasn't demanding—almost as if he'd anticipated rejection.

"Look," he said, pointing over her shoulder as the first fireworks began to explode across the black suede sky.

Giving in to the moment, Amy rested her back against Matt's shoulders, and when she shivered he wrapped his arms around her as if to keep her warm. And to her surprise, it wasn't security and comfort she felt, but instead, a spark of anticipation. The hope of what if. When the bright fireworks thundered and white lights floated across the sky like a weeping willow tree in a summer breeze, her heart felt like it would burst at the seams with feelings she wasn't willing to identify.

Nestled in Matt's arms, Amy would have been content to watch the fireworks for hours, but when the last boom sounded and the red, white and blue lights faded, reality returned. And so did the desire to escape Matt's embrace.

When she turned in his arms to meet his gaze, she saw that he was looking toward the mansion where dancing had begun. Taking her by the hand, he led her to the dance floor and pulled her confidently into his arms. Though she knew she would regret dancing with him when tomorrow dawned, the desire to stay close to him prevailed.

Gliding across the dance floor to the beat of a slow waltz, she could no longer deny her growing attraction to Matt. With her chin resting against his shoulder, her gaze drifted across the friendly crowd as she struggled with her emotions. She thought of how loved and respected Matt was by all his family. Everyone from his parents to Aunt Lila to the youngest Wynn, born only a few months ago, adored this man. Could someone who was admired by so many people be so dangerous to her heart?

No, she thought. Maybe it was time she really got to know Matt Wynn.

As a new song began, Amy felt the promise of a new beginning. She didn't know where this friendship with Matt might lead, but she knew she had to at least open the door and take a peek.

When Tam threw the simple cluster of pale yellow roses, daisies and miniature white carnations tied with lace Aunt Lila had saved from her wedding day, the bridesmaids scrambled to grab hold of tradition. No one was more surprised than Matt when the beautiful bouquet landed in Amy's reluctant hands.

Rubbing the creamy rose petals as if to assure herself the moment was real, Amy accepted her good fortune with a shrug. When well-wishers made boisterous claims that she'd be the next Lexington bride, she laughed as if it were the most ridiculous idea she'd ever heard. But when he saw her search the crowd, stopping only when she met his gaze, he knew something had changed between them.

The shift he'd felt in her posture on the dance floor hadn't been imagined. When she'd danced close to his heart, it was almost as if she'd said, "Handle me with care."

With his gaze still on Amy, he pushed his hands through his hair and whistled softly under his breath. Was it possible he'd misled her? He didn't think so. From the beginning, he'd been clear on his intentions—to help her get her life back on track.

Granted, he'd come to admire her and to enjoy her companionship. And Lord knew he was attracted to her. But what man wouldn't be? She possessed a fresh spirit and a loving heart that touched all she came in contact with.

But she wasn't the one.

He'd known that from the beginning. While they'd formed a unique bond under desperate circumstances, there hadn't been the click in his soul that said, "She's the one God created only for you." And so while he might be tempted by her beauty and her contagious laughter, he wouldn't give in to it. He only had to think of his close friends Gabe and Anna to be reminded of what could go wrong between two people.

Marriage was a sacrament to be taken seriously. When it was good, it was incredible beyond words. But when it soured and fell apart, the devastation was unrelenting. And he never wanted to experience the kind of pain and disillusionment Gabe and Anna had when they'd divorced.

Yet, when Amy's smile widened, he had to close the distance between them.

"How about one more dance before we call it a night?" Only a few guests lingered on the dance floor, as many had already left the beautiful mansion. Amy nodded, placing her hand in Matt's, following him as if she trusted him to never lead her astray.

Swaying to the music, Matt lost himself in the sweet rhythm. With his eyes closed, it was easy to pretend Amy was the one. As if he were at a private slide show, images flashed through his mind. Amy in the herb garden, with the sun in her eyes and dirt streaked across her face. *Click.* Amy running up the hill, laughing as she passed him. *Click.* Amy smiling in disbelief when he told her Leap of Faith was hers to ride. *Click.* The images jumped ahead to the future. Amy in an antique lace dress walking down the aisle toward him. *Click.* The images rushed by. Amy waiting for him to carry her over the threshold. A pregnant Amy glowing with maternal pride and love. Amy cradling his infant son or daughter next to her breast. A gray-haired Amy squeezing his hand as they watched a sunset together. *Click.* The screen went black.

Unnerved by the vivid images, Matt panicked. It was the same old struggle, the secret he never revealed. While he wanted nothing more than to be married and to start a family, he was scared to death of failing as Gabe and Anna had. So scared that he ran every time he got too close to love.

In some ways, he was no different than Amy. They were both afraid of commitment. Ironically, relief followed the realization. What was he getting worked up about, anyway? Amy had made it clear she wouldn't be falling in love for a very long time. If ever. And he believed her. He didn't have any need to worry about what might or might not happen between them.

They said their goodbyes to lingering family and drove the short distance to Aunt Lila's in comfortable silence. With the car windows rolled down and the summer breeze blowing on their faces, they looked like two people without a care in the world.

At the door, Matt said, "I realize tonight wasn't easy for you. And I want you to know, I'm really proud of you."

Amy nodded. "I couldn't have gotten through it without you."

"Yeah, you could have," Matt insisted. "You're much stronger than you think."

"You bring out the best in me," she said. An odd look, which Matt didn't understand, shaded her eyes with regret. "And you survived, yourself."

"Oh, I'm an old hat at this. Besides, with you as my date, I was actually able to enjoy a wedding. In the past, my family has lined up every single woman present. You wouldn't believe the embarrassing moments they've pushed me into."

Amy laughed. "I think I have an idea of what lengths your family would go to. They just want to see you happy. You do so much for them."

He was touched by the thought and barely choked out a thank-you. "That was a nice thing to say."

Amy shrugged, leaning against the porch railing as

if she were in no hurry to end the evening. "It's the truth."

High above, lazy clouds parted over the moon, allowing the bright light to shine on her face. Before he could sensor his thoughts, Matt said, "Do you know how beautiful you are tonight?"

Amy blushed.

"You're more beautiful than the bride was."

Too late he realized he'd said the wrong thing. To any other woman, it would have been a compliment, just as he'd intended it. But to Amy it would be an unwelcome comparison.

"Of course, no one can outshine a bride." Stumbling through the words, he tried to put a new spin on his comment. "It's just that in the moonlight, you're incredibly beautiful."

Amy managed to force a smile and say thank-you, but it was obvious that the closeness they'd shared throughout the evening had ended.

"I never did ask how you came to be in the wedding party," she said. He noticed the defensive look in her eyes before he heard the harsh undertone in her voice.

Matt smiled, grateful the conversation had taken a new direction. "Tam should have anticipated there'd be a problem with Nate as soon as Brittany broke her leg. Nate didn't want to leave Brittany alone at the hospital while all their friends were at the wedding. So he refused to leave her."

"Which put Tam in a bind," Amy guessed.

Matt grimaced. "And guess who the tux fit perfectly?"

Amy's laughter surprised him, and when the amused spark in her eyes spread a warm glow across her face he knew everything was once again okay between them.

Leaning forward, he said, "Just between you and me, Nate has a huge crush on Brittany."

"Like the whole world doesn't know," Amy said.

"I guess it's kind of obvious when two people are in love."

Before he could stop himself, Matt gently rested his hand on her shoulder. Overcome by the urge to kiss her, he blamed his unexpected desire on the talk of love and the moonlight. He quickly pressed his lips against her forehead, just as a good friend might, in an attempt to conceal his longing.

Unable to look her in the eyes for fear he might abandon his good senses, he took her hand and said, "Would you mind praying together before we called it a night?"

"No," Amy said softly, as if she'd lost her breath.

Matt purposely cleared his throat in order to give him a few seconds to think of something suitable to say. But all he could think of was Amy and how beautiful she looked in the moonlight.

"Dear, Lord," he finally began, "thank You for this wonderful night. It's such an honor to celebrate true love in Your presence. May You continue to show us the way You'd have us walk and give us the strength to meet life's challenges. And give Amy guidance and wisdom as she makes decisions concerning her work and where she's to live."

Just as Matt was about to say amen, Amy quickly added, "And Lord, please bless Matt for saving me that day in the convenience store."

When Amy paused, Matt said, "Amen."

Again, he kissed her on the forehead, his lips lingering as they pressed against her baby-soft skin. As he backed away, the strangest sensation washed through him. Even though they stood a few inches apart, he felt as if they were connected, as if in this moment they'd merged into one. He felt closer to her now than he'd felt during the robbery. And he hadn't thought that was possible.

With his mouth suddenly dry, Matt said goodbye. Though he walked calmly to the car and drove down the driveway slowly, once he reached the open highway, he floored the gas pedal. He couldn't get away from Amy fast enough.

Was there a chance he'd been wrong? Was it possible she was the one? If there was the slightest chance, he couldn't risk ruining this growing connection between them.

Amy woke up with the sun, and after grabbing a few bites of toast and a bitter cup of instant coffee, she headed for the stables. Since sleep hadn't eased her frustration, she hoped good old-fashioned work would be her salvation.

For most of the night, she'd replayed the events of the previous evening, trying to make sense of her traitorous emotions. Bouncing the heel of her palm against her forehead, she grimaced. Matt had to know she was attracted to him. She'd been as transparent as a schoolgirl.

But what troubled her even more than her obvious yearnings was the closeness they'd shared as they'd prayed. While the words that had been spoken escaped her memory, the intensity, the closeness she'd felt as she entrusted her hands to his would remain with her forever.

Distracted by her thoughts, Amy finished feeding the horses and sat on the nearest bale of straw. Wiping perspiration from her face with her sleeve, she tried to evaluate the situation objectively. But that was impossible. There was nothing objective about her feelings for Matt Wynn. In fact, if she didn't know better she'd think she was in love with the man.

"But that's impossible," she said out loud, to herself and to any horses that cared to listen.

"What's impossible?" Matt asked.

Amy nearly jumped off the bale of straw when he approached. "You promised me you wouldn't sneak up on me again," she said.

"That's a promise I can't keep," he said.

A promise I can't keep. As the words echoed through her mind the situation became very clear. But where she expected relief, an anger fueled by disappointment and regret charged through her.

"I'm sure you can't." She threw the words at him as if they had the power to burn.

"Now what's that supposed to mean?" The carefree look on Matt's face vanished, and displeasure surfaced in its place.

"You know exactly what it means. Or at least you should. You don't have what you want, Matt, because you don't make promises you're afraid to keep."

When anger crept into his eyes, she realized he understood. However, his pride refused to let him admit he didn't have the wife and children he so desperately desired because he was too afraid to make a commitment. Why he was so afraid she wasn't certain.

"Look, Matt, forget I said anything. I'm just rambling. I didn't get much sleep last night."

"No, I don't want to let this go."

"Well, you're going to have to figure it out on your own, then, because I'm going in to shower and change for church."

With the firm declaration, Amy left Matt in the stable. Once she reached the house, she ran for her room, passing Lila on the wide stairway. When Lila didn't try to stop her, she knew she must have looked a fright.

She shouldn't have spoken so boldly to Matt. It wasn't her place. Just because she'd embarrassed herself with him the night before didn't give her the right to lash out at him. But she knew what she was doing. She was pushing him away before he discovered how deep her feelings ran. Because the honest truth was that despite her intentions, she'd let him get too close to her heart. When or where he'd slipped in, she didn't know. She couldn't remain on the Wynn farm much longer, and as long as she did, she had to keep her distance from him.

Falling to her knees in prayer, Amy closed her eyes and asked God to please show her what step she needed to take next.

Help me not to act out of my own selfishness, but to consider the needs of those around me.

She sat in silence for a long time, listening for the voice of God. And when she did hear it, it wasn't what she wanted to hear at all. She needed to go home to Ohio. In order to forgive Garry, she had to face him. Unless she did, the bitterness would eventually destroy her and those she loved.

Oh, God, Amy cried with shameful honesty. *I'm just not ready to let go of all the pain and anger.*

Chapter Twelve

Amy didn't have to worry about avoiding Matt, because for the next two days she didn't even catch a glimpse of him. And when their paths did finally cross in the stable, he nodded at her and kept walking. Though she was getting exactly what she wanted, she didn't like it.

His aloofness made her realize how much she'd come to enjoy their conversations. As she saddled Leap of Faith and rode across the meadow, she wished Matt could have been at her side. But it wasn't to be, and it was best she got used to it.

She rode to the far end of the property and back and was almost home when her cell phone rang. Bringing Faith to a quick stop, she answered. "You've got a letter from your mother," Lila said. "I thought it might be important."

"I'll be right in," Amy said, because she knew if she didn't go, it would cause Lila needless concern.

By the time Amy groomed Faith and reached the house, she found Lila and Matt sitting in a shady spot on the veranda. She should have suspected Lila might have an agenda of her own.

"Matt smelled the sugar cookies baking," Lila said with a smile that convinced Amy she was extremely pleased with herself.

"As good as your cookies are, it's a wonder half the county isn't here." Amy saw no point in letting Lila know she'd caught on to her well-meaning tricks.

And just as Amy feared, as soon as she was seated and sipped her iced tea, Lila handed her the letter and made an excuse to leave.

"It's been a long day," she said. "I think I'll take a short nap before dinner."

Matt stood, helping Lila to her feet. "You're not overdoing it, are you?"

Lila shook her head, assuring her worried nephew. "I'm trying to get a head start on Cara and Paul's wedding. It'll be here before we know it."

"If you're certain you're okay," Matt persisted.

Lila nodded. "But it would make me happy to know you'll join us for dinner tonight. Amy fixed a huge pan of lasagna, and I know how you love Italian food."

Amy saw the conflicting emotions flood Matt's eyes. In the end, he chose not to disappoint his aunt. "Of course, I'd love to stay. It sure beats going home to an empty house and a frozen dinner."

"That's exactly what I said to Amy this morning.

See you later, then," Lila said as she disappeared through the doorway.

Matt sighed. "I'm sorry about that. I couldn't turn her down without causing a scene."

"You know she's trying to set us up," Amy said.

"Only since the day she met you."

"But then I'm sure she tries to match you up with every pretty girl she meets."

An uneasy look crossed Matt's face, and he glanced away. "Actually, you're the first woman she's seriously—"

Before Matt could finish the sentence, Amy interrupted. "I think the easiest thing to do is to just play along with her plans. There's no use fighting her."

Matt smiled. "That'd be like hitting a brick wall at a hundred miles an hour."

Out of nervousness, Amy laughed. But it was an awkward pitch that surely betrayed her uneasiness with the conversation.

"Don't worry, I'll be leaving soon," Amy said.

Matt looked at the letter on the table, the return address legible at the close distance. "Will you be going back to Ohio?"

Amy shook her head. "Not permanently."

"For a visit then?" he asked.

Though she knew he wasn't prying but merely trying to make conversation, the question still irritated her. Her plans were none of his business. She'd be his date to the last family wedding, and then as soon as she was certain Lila was fine on her own, she'd move into her own place.

But why, when she thought of moving out and finding a great job, did the screen in her mind go black? Why could she only see herself in this house, on this piece of land that had been in the Wynn family for five generations?

"I'll go home sometime this summer." She answered Matt's question.

"Don't let me stop you from reading the letter." He slowly took a sip of iced tea.

Somehow she knew he wasn't leaving until she'd read the letter and so she ripped it open and skimmed the same plea her mother wrote in all her letters.

"Your father and I miss you, and we'd love to see you. Please, come home soon. And don't forget the Jenkins family reunion is the third weekend of July. Everyone will be asking about you, so why don't you come home for the weekend? You know how much you love seeing your cousins."

Amy skipped to the bottom of the letter and then stopped.

"If you don't come home soon, we'll plan to visit Lexington the week after the reunion. Your father has several vacation days left, and we haven't been to Lexington in ages. And we'd love to meet Lila and see the Wynn horse farm. From the few times we've talked to her on the telephone, I know we'll love her."

Amy's gaze skipped over the lawn to the far pasture, and she watched the group of frisky thoroughbreds gallop across the bluegrass pasture toward a shady stand of trees. Their beauty mesmerized her for a moment, allowing a brief respite from the problem at hand. There was a part of her that wanted her parents to see the beauty of this farm, but she knew it was too soon. They weren't coming to see the rolling hills or Lila's herb garden or the inspiring clock tower that set the pace of her day. No, they were coming to take her home. To them, her stay in Lexington was nothing more than a silly indulgence they tolerated.

Either way, it was a no-win situation. She didn't want to go home, but neither did she want her parents to come to Lexington. Perhaps she could meet them halfway. No, they'd never settle for that.

"Anything I can help with?" Matt asked.

Amy shook her head.

"I'm a good listener," he added.

Slowly but surely, Amy felt her resolve to keep Matt at a safe distance dissolve under her need to talk about the letter.

"My parents are thinking about visiting at the end of the month," she explained.

"That's great. I'd love to meet them. I'm sure Aunt Lila would host a family barbecue in their honor. They could meet the entire family. I'm sure my parents would even drive down from Louisville."

Amy glared at Matt.

"And that's not a good idea?" The wrinkles in his brows deepened as he cocked his head in disbelief.

"No, it's complicated. You know that."

"Is it really?" Matt asked. "Let me see if I can't sum up the situation. Your parents have always been overprotective and since you've left they've been even more worried about you than usual. But you're afraid if they make the trip out here, they'll cause a scene and insist you go home with them."

Amy had to admit he'd said it better than she could have.

"None of this would be a problem if you knew what you wanted to do. So what are you going to do, Amy? Are you staying in Lexington or are you leaving me?"

Leaving me.

He stared at her, unwilling to look away until she answered him. It was obvious, though, by the steadiness of his gaze that he wasn't aware of the slip he'd made. Did this mean he didn't want her to leave? And should that make a difference to her?

"I don't know what I'm going to do," she finally said. "But I can't see myself moving back there. It feels as if Ohio belongs to a different lifetime." *And I feel as if I belong here,* she thought.

"Compromise," he suggested. "Go back for a visit. Assure your parents you're okay. Let them see how happy you are. Convince them this is where you belong."

He spoke with a conviction that unnerved her and yet at the same time gave her hope for the future. And in that hope there was a bubble of clarity. God had brought Matt into her life. From the moment he'd held her in the closet, she'd had no doubt of that. Now she knew why. When she'd met Matt, she was lost in disillusionment and despair, content to wallow in her self-pity. But little by little, Matt had reintroduced her to joy, companionship, and paved the way for her to rebuild her trust in God. He'd shown her the reasons to leave her pain behind and to move on. He'd helped her see there was a beautiful future ahead for her, though it was up to her to embrace it.

God had sent Matt into her life when she'd needed him most. For that she would always be grateful. But they weren't a match. They weren't destined to build a future or a family together. They'd been brought together for a reason, to bring out the best in each other. She could only hope she'd somehow affected Matt's life as deeply as he'd touched hers.

"There's a family reunion in a week," Amy said softly. "They'd like me to come."

"It sounds like the perfect solution," Matt said.

"I don't know." Amy picked up a sugar cookie and nibbled.

The thought of going back to Ohio terrified her. There'd be no shelter in her hometown, no place where she could run from the past. She'd have to look her hurt and anger in the eye and crush it. But did she have the strength to do that?

As if Matt could read her mind, he leaned forward and took her hand. Instantly, the seed of hope grew. As far as her heart was concerned there would never be a good time to go home.

"You've made it through two weddings, and you didn't think you'd be able to do that," he encouraged.

"But you were with me," Amy said, letting the

words slip out before she could consider their significance.

"The strength came from within," Matt insisted, unwilling to accept any credit.

"I'll think about it," Amy promised.

"I think you know what you have to do," Matt said. "But it's your choice."

Amy pinched the crisp sugar cookie between her fingers so tightly it crumbled.

The telephone rang just as Amy and Lila returned from their morning prayer walk.

"Whew, that felt good," Lila said as she hurried toward the telephone. With a wink, she added, "It's such a blessing to feel like my young self again."

"I don't know if I can keep up with you anymore," Amy teased. However, there was a kernel of truth in her words. With every day that passed, Lila's stamina doubled if not tripled.

On the fourth ring, Lila answered the telephone. "Well, hello, it's nice to hear from you this morning."

Amy listened until she was certain the call wasn't for her. Ever since her mother's letter had arrived several days ago, she'd jumped each time the phone rang or a car drove up. She knew if she didn't talk to her mother soon, her parents would take matters into their own hands.

After taking a quick shower and changing into Capri pants and a knit top, Amy went downstairs to fix a light breakfast. She was surprised to see Lila was still on the telephone, and even more surprised when Lila covered one end of the receiver with her hand and quietly said, "Your mother wants to talk to you."

Amy's heart sank to her feet.

"Amy just walked in the room," Lila said into the receiver. "I promise, we're taking good care of her. Yes, it was good to talk to you, too, Luanne. Please assure your husband everything is fine."

Lila offered a supportive smile as she passed Amy the telephone receiver.

"Hello, Mom," Amy said in her most confident voice. "Yes, I got your letter. No, there's no need for you and Daddy to drive all this way. I'll come see you. No, not this weekend. Maybe for the reunion. There's just so much going on here, and I'm not certain when I can get away. I love you, too, Mom. Yes, I miss you, and I promise, I'll come home soon."

Having lost her appetite, Amy left the kitchen and went straight to the herb garden where she began pulling weeds and tilling the rich soil. Not until sweat rolled down both sides of her face did she wipe her brow and cheeks with the blue bandana she carried in her back pocket. Leaning back on her heels and stretching out the kinks in her back, she allowed herself to think about the conversation with her mother.

She did miss her parents. And she missed the friends and family she'd left behind. Maybe enough time had passed. Maybe there wouldn't be sympathetic looks from well-intentioned friends. Maybe they wouldn't whisper behind her back any longer. Maybe they'd no longer treat her like a fragile doll.

After all, she wasn't the first bride in history to be jilted and survive.

Who was she kidding?

"I didn't know you were such a chicken."

"Did I hear you correctly?" When Matt's gaze continued to challenge her, she threw the book she'd been reading at him. Lila had obviously told him Amy still hadn't picked a date to go home.

"I was having a very nice evening until you arrived."

It had been a long day, and Amy was exhausted. After working most of the morning in the herb garden, she'd let Lila talk her into accompanying her to the organizational meeting for vacation bible school, which would be held later in the summer at the church she attended with Lila. When Lila had volunteered Amy as a teacher, Amy couldn't say no. Because the meeting had stretched into the late afternoon, she'd had to race home to finish her stable chores before fixing a healthy meal for Lila. As soon as the last dish was dried and Lila had settled into her favorite reading chair, Amy planted herself on the veranda intending to relax in solitude.

Matt picked up the book she'd tossed and examined it. "I take it you're going to enroll in the fall semester," he said, as he handed the university catalogue to her.

"That's the plan." Though there were still a lot of details to work out. The primary one being money. Having declared her independence, she couldn't expect her parents to support her financially. But after meeting with the university counselor, she was hopeful that between loans and the right job she could at least afford to start as a part-time student in the fall. And there was always the chance she'd receive a scholarship.

"It sounds like you're on the right track," he said.

"I don't know." Amy turned the book over and over in her hands. "Why is it so hard for me to decide what I want to do with my life?" Because she really didn't want him to answer, she continued, "I went to school with kids who knew in elementary school that they wanted to be a doctor, or a teacher, or to own their own business when they grew up. Why is this so hard for me?"

Matt shook his head and offered a slight shrug. "Who am I to say what God has planned for your life? But I know from my own experience that when I'm having trouble making a decision, the answer is usually staring me in the face."

"Oh, that's a lot of help," Amy said. The only thing staring her in the face was Matt Wynn, and he was part of the problem, not the solution.

Matt moved closer, and Amy took a step backward only to bump into a porch column. "You know what I think?" he asked.

"What?" she said, only because he was determined to share his opinion.

"I think the reason you can't decide what to do at the end of the summer is that you're afraid of failing."

Amy leaned back her head and laughed. Not because what Matt said was funny, but because it was the most hypocritical thing he'd ever said to her.

"Who are you talking to?" she asked, not caring if she made him angry. "Me or yourself?"

"I don't know what you mean." Though he pretended ignorance, she noticed the slight quiver of his lip and the way he'd shoved his hands into his jeans pockets.

"Of course you do," she said. This time, she moved toward him, backing him up against the house wall. "You talk about your dreams of a wife and children, and the reason you don't have either is that the idea of making a commitment scares you silly. You run every time you get close to a woman you could fall in love with."

Taking a side step, Matt momentarily escaped the wrath of her gaze. "What does it matter to you?"

"It doesn't," she claimed. "But the next time you point your finger at me, you'd better take a good hard look at your own heart."

"You know it doesn't matter what's going on in my life, the facts are still the same. You're afraid to let anyone close. And not just a man. You keep everyone at a safe distance—Lila, your parents, my family, your friends back home. You haven't let anyone close for a long time. And that's no way to live."

Overwrought, Amy sat in the nearest chair. What he said was true. While she'd been aware of her need to avoid even the hint of romantic involvement with anyone, she hadn't realized the wall she'd built around her heart had also protected her from everyone who truly cared for her.

"How could I have done that?" she asked, as much to God as she did to Matt.

Kneeling beside her, he said, "You did what you had to do at the time. But you don't need that wall any longer."

"You're right," she admitted. "I have to go home—and soon."

Matt exhaled loudly, as if her decision affected him as much as it did her.

"Let's make a deal. If you'll face your fears, I'll face mine."

She smiled. "You don't have anything to worry about. You'll know when the right woman comes along, because she'll melt your fears away."

Matt lifted her hand to his lips and kissed it. "You're much wiser and stronger than you think."

"You bring that out in me," she said.

"I'll tell you…" Matt glanced away before he finished the sentence, as if he might regret voicing the thought.

"Tell me what?" Amy prodded.

Taking a deep breath, Matt said, "I'll go to the reunion with you. After all, it's the least I can do after you've agreed to suffer through three family weddings with me."

"You don't know what you're getting into." The offer brought a small smile to Amy's lips, and she knew she should turn him down. His presence would only complicate her trip.

"I think I know exactly what I'm doing," Matt assured her.

"Okay," Amy finally agreed. "You've got a date to a family reunion."

Suddenly, going home didn't seem like such a bad idea.

Chapter Thirteen

"Come on, Amy," Matt called, "it's time to leave."

Amy rushed toward him, dropped her suitcase by the car trunk, then headed toward the stables. "Give me five more minutes," she yelled. "We can make up the time on the road."

Matt loaded her overnight bag into his car, then headed for Leap of Faith's stall. By the time he caught up with Amy, she had her head buried in the mare's mane and her arms wrapped around her neck. Faith's sad eyes suggested that even she was aware of the significance of the trip.

After a few minutes, he grabbed Amy by the elbows and gently pulled her away. Faith shook her head, then released a sorrowful whinny. Slipping from his grasp, Amy ran to the horse. Anyone watching might have thought she was saying goodbye to the proud mare.

She was saying goodbye.

The thought gripped and twisted his heart until he couldn't breathe. Amy might never come home. When Matt's gaze drifted down the stall-lined aisle, he found that all the horses had turned toward Amy as if to express their own goodbyes.

Suddenly, he saw images of Amy everywhere in the stable. He saw her carrying buckets of water that were so heavy they weighed her shoulders down. He saw her wipe her brow with her sleeve as she brushed Faith until the mare's black coat was sleek and shiny. He heard her humming softly as she rubbed the pungent saddle soap into the saddle his grandmother had once ridden. He heard her laughing as she mucked out stalls. Never again would he walk into this stable without seeing her.

Yet, somehow he had to say goodbye, too.

Now that he finally understood why God had brought Amy into his life, he didn't trust himself to carry out the deed. He couldn't imagine never seeing her smile again or watching her ride across the bluegrass pastures on Faith with her hair flying in the wind.

Why, God? he silently cried.

For reasons Matt would never fully understand, he believed God trusted him to see Amy safely returned to her family. He should never have grown so close to her, because when he said goodbye, she would take a chunk of his heart with her.

But who was he to doubt God's plans?

"Amy," he said. "It's time."

When she glanced at him with timid eyes, he wanted to squeeze her until she promised she'd never leave.

"Let's go," she said, placing her hand in his as they started for the car.

For the first time he could ever remember, Matt didn't feel the peace that came from doing the right thing.

From a block away, Amy spotted her parents sitting on the front porch.

She groaned. "How embarrassing."

"What is?" Matt asked.

"I've got a welcoming committee," she said, pointing to the one-story brick home with the terraced lawn and beautiful flower beds.

"And you're complaining? If more parents cared about their kids like yours do, the world would be a lot better."

"Yeah, there'd be a lot more runaways."

When Matt frowned in the same way Lila would have, she said, "I'm sorry. It was a bad joke. I'm just edgy. I love my parents. Really."

From the moment she'd left the Lexington city limits, she'd been restless and tense. To make matters worse, she and Matt had barely spoken during the long drive.

Before she opened the car door, she turned to him, "Listen, if you don't want to stay, I'll understand."

She watched the struggle in his eyes and knew he was going to desert her. Biting her bottom lip, she promised herself she wouldn't beg him to stay. She could get through this weekend on her own.

As her parents approached the car, bright smiles plastered on their faces, Amy said, "Well?"

"I'm staying," Matt said, though he didn't sound too sure of himself.

Before any more could be said, Mr. Jenkins opened the car door and shook Matt's hand while his wife hugged Amy until she couldn't breathe.

"How are you? Turn around. Let me look at you. You're tanned. You look wonderful. Have you lost weight? Are you tired after the long drive? How about a sandwich or would you rather take a nap? I'm fixing your favorites for dinner—cold chicken pasta salad and strawberry shortcake." The words bubbled out of Luanne's heart as if she hadn't seen her daughter for a year instead of only two short months.

After hugging her mother long and hard, Amy followed her father and Matt into the house. While her parents showed Matt to the guest bedroom, Amy lingered in her girlhood room. Her souvenirs of a happy childhood—dolls, a dozen well-hugged teddy bears, her favorite Grace Livingston Hill books, dried prom corsages—were all exactly as she'd left them.

Down the hallway, she could hear her father and Matt talking. They'd already found a common interest in baseball and were enjoying an argument over whether or not the Reds would win the pennant and be the favorites in the World Series come fall.

"You know they could talk about baseball for

hours.'' Her mother stood in the doorway as if she were afraid of intruding.

"Daddy loves his Cincinnati Reds,'' Amy said. It felt good to be home where the noises and the scents were familiar.

"He's a nice young man,'' Luanne said.

"He comes from a wonderful family.'' Amy picked up a teddy bear and retied the faded satin ribbon around its neck.

"He's quite good-looking,'' her mother persisted, stepping into the room.

"Mom,'' Amy said, finally picking up on her mother's not-so-subtle insinuation. "We're just friends.'' Amy spoke clearly and slowly so there'd be no room for doubt.

"For now,'' Luanne said. "But if things were to change down the road—''

"Mother,'' Amy said firmly.

Luanne pressed her fists against her waist in a frustrated fashion. "I promised myself I wouldn't do this. You're not even home a half hour and already I'm—''

"Shh,'' Amy said. "You don't have to apologize.'' Those were not words Amy was accustomed to saying to her mother.

"But I do,'' Luanne insisted. "I need to apologize for how I treated you after the wedding was called off. I don't know if I'll ever be able to forgive myself for the thoughtless things I said to you.''

The sincere regret in Luanne's voice brought tears to Amy's eyes. "It's all in the past,'' Amy assured her. It was enough that she still clung to the pain of

Garry's betrayal. There was no reason for her mother and father to suffer, as well.

"No, I think it's still between us. I'm part of the reason you packed up and left. I drove you away."

When Amy tried to interrupt, her mother spoke louder and faster.

"I was so caught up in the wedding I didn't stop to think what a horrible thing Garry had done. I should never have told you he was just acting out a case of cold feet and that you should forgive him and forget it ever happened."

Hearing the advice now, it sounded coldhearted, but at the time Amy knew her mother had been trapped by volatile emotions and wedding plans that had spun out of control.

"The wedding was only a few days away. We'd already opened wedding gifts and out-of-town family had started to arrive. My dress had been altered and my bridal portrait was hanging on the living room wall."

Luanne shook her head. "It doesn't matter. I let you down. Can you ever forgive me?"

Tears flowed down Luanne's face, and within seconds Amy wrapped her arms around her mother's soft body. Home wasn't a place, she thought. Home was anywhere you could embrace love.

After a few minutes, Luanne lifted Amy's chin with her fingers so she could look into her daughter's eyes.

"How are you really doing?" she asked.

"I'm fine," Amy said.

"You have to forgive yourself," Luanne said softly with wisdom rooted in a deep faith.

"I'm working on it," Amy promised.

"If I can help—"

"You already have." Amy hugged her mother again. She sensed this was a new beginning for them and reveled in the closeness. Her mother no longer saw her as a child, but as a young woman, and that bolstered Amy's self-confidence in ways she hadn't expected.

"We'd better join the men before your daddy comes looking for you," Luanne said.

"I'll be there in a moment," Amy promised.

Alone, she knelt beside her bed and asked God to please give Garry the good sense not to show at the reunion.

The family reunion, as it was every year, was at the west pavilion at the park by the lake. Amy rose early and helped her mother prepare the traditional baked beans, deviled eggs and strawberry cake. Since her father was chief barbecuer, they arrived at the park early to start the charcoal fires. The chicken, which had marinated in huge plastic tubs, sizzled as it hit the hot grills.

"Mm," Matt said. "It doesn't get any better than this."

Amy punched him playfully in the arm and said, "You'd probably say the same thing about hot dogs."

"Well, there's nothing better than a grilled hot dog

with mustard and..." Matt's voice faded to silence when Amy shook her head.

"My point exactly," she said.

They sat on a blanket not far from the grills and tables, enjoying what might be their last quiet moment before the rest of the family arrived.

"Are you ready to meet the Jenkins clan?" she asked when the first two cars pulled up and a half dozen kids jumped out and ran for the play area.

"Compared to my family, this ought to be a piece of cake."

"You said that, not me."

Matt stood, then extended his hand. She accepted, enjoying the brief comfort his warm grip offered as he pulled her to her feet. As if they'd landed in a swarm of bees, family gathered around them to welcome Amy home and to meet the handsome man at her side.

For what seemed like the hundredth time, she said to Justin, a cousin who had arrived late and immediately made the wrong assumption, "I work for Matt's aunt. We're just friends."

After Justin walked away, Matt said, "They don't believe us. Maybe it'd be easier to pretend we're a couple than to convince them otherwise."

At first, Amy scrunched her nose at the idea, but then she conceded. "I'm afraid you're right."

Still, she jumped the first time he put his arm around her waist.

"Relax," he whispered. And when his moist breath caressed her neck she felt an unexpected calmness.

Touch by touch—a hand on her shoulder, a touch on the small of her back, a playful pat on the top of her head—she began to enjoy herself and forget about Garry.

The afternoon passed quickly. Everyone agreed that her daddy's chicken was even better than the year before, and the aunts argued over whether it was safer to wait a half hour or an hour before swimming. Not until everyone was sunburned and tuckered out from softball, volleyball and swimming did they congregate at the pavilion.

By this time, the sun had lost its sting and appetites had returned. Food that had been stored in ice chests, along with a new round of soft drinks and frozen fruit pops were passed out. As everyone, young and old, settled down in a circle, guitars were pulled from cases and the singing began.

"This is my favorite part of the reunion," Amy whispered to Matt. Her uncle Bob, the unofficial bandleader, could play everything from *Barney* songs to pop standards to favorite hymns.

"Things are winding down, then," Matt said, with a disappointment that pleased Amy. All in all, she couldn't have asked for a more lovely day.

She laughed, then said, "This is just the beginning of the end. Uncle Bob can play for hours. There's still the bonfire and s'mores to look forward to."

When Matt leaned closer and kissed Amy on the top of the head, she felt the blush rise in her cheeks. Out of the corner of her eye, she caught the knowing look on her mother's face.

"What was that for?" she asked, thinking he'd taken their plan to let everyone believe they were a couple a little too far.

"I just wanted to thank-you for a great day. I'm really glad I had the chance to meet your family and to see where you grew up. It makes me understand you better."

"According to my mother, that's an impossible task at times," Amy quipped, only because the intimate nature of their conversation made her uneasy. Though they sat on a quilt in the midst of forty or fifty relatives, they might as well have been stranded on their own private island.

"Well, I have a feeling your mother and you are going to get along much better in the future."

Amy nodded. "I was silly to put off coming home for so long. Everyone's been wonderful. No one's even mentioned the wedding or..." She didn't want to say his name and spoil a perfectly splendid afternoon.

"What did you expect?" Matt asked.

"I'm not sure. I guess because I felt so stupid and foolish, I believed everyone else would judge me as harshly. I thought I'd be the jilted bride forever in their minds. I didn't have the courage to look them in the eyes, and as it turns out, all they wanted to do was give me a hug and tell me everything would be all right."

Matt kept his voice low as the singing began. "Maybe something good has come out of this."

"What?" Amy asked with genuine interest.

"I think you've realized how important family is. And not just your parents and your grandparents, but your extended family, as well." Matt paused as Amy's gaze drifted across the generations, then rested on her grandmothers, who sat in lawn chairs on the opposite side of the bonfire.

When Matt brushed the hair from her shoulder, Amy's attention returned to him. "I'm glad you've had this chance to reconnect with them," he said. "The older I get, the more I value my family and realize how much I truly need them. I can't imagine my life without Aunt Lila's wisdom, my mother's love or my father's perspective. Life is so much fuller and meaningful when you can share it with people you love…with people you've grown up with…with people who know your history."

As Amy listened to Matt, she couldn't help but feel he was trying to tell her something that transcended the obvious meaning of his words. It was almost as if he were preparing her for something, but what she didn't know.

Deciding she was reading too much into his tone, Amy let the idea go and joined in with the singing. As the sun dropped below the horizon, she sighed inwardly, thankful her worries about Garry had been for nothing.

It wasn't until the last song had been sung and the bonfire doused with water that she heard the crunch of gravel. In the darkness, the bright headlights prevented her from clearly seeing the car. But she didn't have to see the blue sports utility vehicle to know it was Garry.

Still, that didn't mean she had to talk to him. In this crowd of people, with everyone scurrying to carry ice chests, leftover bags of chips and sports equipment to their cars, it would be easy to avoid her former fiancé and her cousin.

Amy was only a few feet from Matt's car, a few feet from being home free, when someone called Garry's name. Instantly, Matt froze, and before she realized what he was doing he steered her away from the car and directly into the path of Garry and Rhonda.

What kind of game did he think he was playing? She pinched his arm so he'd know how angry she was with his little ploy.

"Hello, Amy." Garry and Rhonda spoke in unison.

"Hi," Amy answered. When Matt poked her in the side, she stammered, "I'd like you to meet my friend, Matt Wynn."

This time she didn't emphasize that he was her employer's nephew, nor that they were just friends. If Garry and Rhonda made the wrong assumptions, it was fine with her.

"I'm glad we ran into you," Garry said.

She knew by the nervous dip of his chin that he wanted this awkward moment to be over as quickly as she did.

"Our paths are bound to cross. It's a small town," Amy conceded. "Plus, you're dating my cousin."

"We're really sorry, Amy," Rhonda said. "We didn't mean to hurt you."

When Matt's arm tightened around her waist, Amy was grateful for the support. Without looking, she knew her parents, aunts and uncles and cousins were watching with burning curiosity. And that caused her to realize that her actions would send a lasting ripple throughout the family.

Forcing a smile to her face, she said, "I'm happy for you both. On the chance you didn't come earlier today on my account, I want you to know that won't be necessary in the future. I think this family is big enough for us all."

As she spoke, Amy felt a measure of peace envelop her body. Though she'd been forced into this moment by Matt, she believed she'd handled it well. Daring to stare at Garry until he met her gaze, she was amazed that she no longer felt the raw hurt or pain that had nearly crippled her heart.

No, the love she'd felt for Garry had died the instant she'd caught him kissing Rhonda. And now she knew her heart was truly beginning to heal. It felt so good to stand before him and know with certainty that he wasn't the man God had chosen for her to marry. That if she'd married Garry she would have made the biggest mistake of her life. So, in an odd way, she was thankful he'd screwed up.

Since there was nothing left to say, Amy turned to Matt and said, "It's time to go."

She might not have anything more to say to Garry, but she had plenty to say to Matt.

* * *

It wasn't until they were in the car that Matt fully understood how upset Amy was.

"How could you?" she shouted as soon as the car doors were shut. "Who gave you the right to play God tonight?"

Realizing she was too angry to listen to his explanation, he let her rage tumble out during the short drive to her parents' home.

"You had no right to interfere. What did you think a confrontation would accomplish? What if it hadn't gone well? You could have ruined the whole reunion for everyone."

Matt pulled into the driveway and cut the engine. When Amy started to get out, he grabbed her by the arm and stopped her. "I think we should finish this conversation now. I don't think you want to include your parents in this."

"There's nothing more to say." Her eyes burned with a fire he'd never seen before. Until that moment, he hadn't realized how deeply Garry's betrayal had hurt her. And that convinced him that he'd been right to bring her home. She was starting to heal on the surface, but those wounds ran far deeper than even she realized. Only here, in Ohio, surrounded by her family could she heal.

Sucking in air, Matt felt as if he'd been punched. Things were clearer for him, too. Amy wasn't the one. Her fragile heart was a long way from being able to love in the way he wanted and needed to be loved by a wife.

"Maybe nothing more for you to say, because you've done all the talking since we left the park."

Crossing her arms over her chest, Amy stared out the window, a disgusted look shielding her face.

"I know you're angry with me now. But someday, you'll thank me for forcing you to confront Garry. The longer you put it off the harder it would be…and I couldn't bear the thought of you never facing him."

Turning her head with his fingers, he challenged her teary eyes to look at him. "Now you can get on with the business of getting over him. Now you can move on with your life."

He could tell by the light in her eyes that she knew he was right, though she wouldn't admit it to him tonight. Instead she said, "But you didn't have any right to take my choice away."

He understood the heart of her anger. "There's a fine line between being independent and accepting help," he said, then he sighed. "Okay, so maybe I did step over the line. But please believe me when I say I only had your best interests at heart."

When he saw the tear slip from her eye, he thought his heart would break into a million pieces. Overwhelmed with the need to comfort her, he stroked her cheek lightly with his hand, and when she pressed her chin against his palm, he reached out to her. He drew her into his arms, and his lips hovered over hers, giving her a chance to back away. When she didn't, he kissed her. The sweetness of her lips was everything he'd dreamed it could be. But instead of leaving him satisfied, it only made him yearn for more. And he knew he couldn't have more.

Instantly, Amy tensed, then pulled away. He saw the fear in her eyes and he knew the ties that had bound them together since the hour they'd spent in the convenience store closet had finally snapped. God had brought them together, and now it was time they went their separate ways. Matt had done all he could do for Amy. The rest was up to her.

Alone in her childhood bedroom, Amy clutched her teddy bear and cried. Never in her life had she felt such deep and intense pain. And it had nothing to do with Garry, but everything to do with Matt. She had fallen in love with the man who had saved her life. But while he'd been able to rescue her from danger, he hadn't been able to overcome the damage Garry had inflicted.

She'd been naive to think that one confrontation would erase all the hurt and anger that had festered during the last weeks. The simple truth was that even though she'd forgiven Garry, she hadn't forgotten how he'd hurt her. Loving someone new was still too risky for her damaged heart.

Though Amy knew her parents sensed the tension between her and Matt, she was grateful they didn't ask questions. They attended church and dinner at her grandmother's as if they were one happy family.

It wasn't until after her parents had retired for the evening that Matt mentioned he needed to talk to her.

Naturally, she assumed he wanted to touch base on what time they'd leave for Lexington the following morning. When he stepped onto the patio, she knew he had something more serious on his mind. Something he didn't want her parents to overhear.

"Please, Amy," he said, when she didn't follow. "This will only take a moment."

Swallowing hard, she shut the sliding glass door behind her. Crossing to the opposite side of the deck, she put as much distance between them as possible. But not too much, because she didn't want him to have to talk loud enough for the neighbors to hear.

"I'm leaving at eight tomorrow," he said.

"Fine. I'll be ready. I won't keep you waiting." Her thoughts instantly shifted to Leap of Faith, and how she'd delayed their trip to Ohio because she'd hated to leave her newfound friend. Just the thought of Faith brought a smile to her face. As soon as she got home, she was going for a ride.

Matt looked away, as if he found it difficult to speak. "You don't understand," he said. "*I'm* going home tomorrow," he repeated.

"Oh," Amy said, understanding on the second try.

"You belong here with your family. This is your home," he said.

Amy shook her head. "There you go again, making decisions for me. Yes, this is where I grew up, but I live in Lexington now." Though she loved her parents and this small town, it was no longer home. "I'm going back with you in the morning," Amy insisted.

"You're just saying that out of a sense of obligation and duty. You don't owe me anything for what happened in the convenience store. We saved each other. As far as I'm concerned, we're even."

"But I promised Aunt Lila—"

"We both know Aunt Lila is well enough to live on her own again. She won't ask you to leave the farm, though, because she's clinging to some fairy-tale hope that we'll fall in love and…" Matt left the sentence unfinished.

"And we both know that's not going to happen, right?" She needed to be clear on this.

"Right," Matt agreed.

Amy paced across the deck, quickly trying to organize her feelings. "I'm still coming back, and it's not out of a sense of obligation. I'm coming back because I know in my heart Lexington is where God wants me to be." She'd never been so certain of anything in her life.

Matt shrugged. "I think you're making a huge mistake. Until you can completely forgive Garry, you'll never be able to move on with your life. And you need to be here to do that." Matt opened the patio door, but before he left her alone with her thoughts, he said, "If you really meant what you said, then Lexington will wait for you."

Amy watched Matt's back until he disappeared down the hallway and she heard the soft click of the guest room door. She swallowed hard. Had he been telling her that he would wait for her? No, that couldn't have been what he meant.

Chapter Fourteen

Matt quietly left the Jenkins home, locked the front door behind him and threw his overnight bag into the trunk before anyone discovered he'd gone. Just before five in the morning, the sleepy neighborhood was dark and silent except for the rhythmic hiss of lawn sprinklers and the thud of newspapers smacking driveways.

He was doing the right thing, he told himself as he turned onto the highway. Deep down, Amy knew he was right. He'd seen it in her eyes. She was just too stubborn to admit she belonged in Ohio with her friends and family. Lexington had merely been a temporary home for her. She was stronger now, and thanks to the time she'd spent with Aunt Lila, ready to overcome her fears.

In a few hours, she'd find the brief note he'd left her. Knowing she'd be concerned about her car and belongings, he'd promised to have them driven back to Ohio as soon as possible. He wished her well and encouraged her to keep in touch with Aunt Lila. The only thing he hadn't been able to say was goodbye.

As the miles passed, Matt could no longer fight back the tears. He couldn't let go of the feeling that for a few short weeks his dreams had been within reach.

Amy woke early and was surprised to find her parents already drinking coffee at the kitchen table. Their solemn faces, combined with the nervous glances they exchanged, immediately convinced her something was terribly wrong.

Panicked, she ran to the front window. Matt wouldn't leave without her. But his car was gone. She tried to tell herself he'd just gone to get gas. Nothing else would be open this early.

"He left you a note," her mother said, handing Amy a small envelope.

Reality quickly sunk in. Matt had left her. He'd abandoned her just as Garry had. Amy couldn't believe this was happening to her again. Why couldn't she have learned her lesson the first time?

She slipped her fingers under the flap and broke the seal. Determined to hide her humiliation from her parents, she casually said, "We talked last night. I'm going to stay over a few more days. I'll rent a car for the drive back to Lexington. The weekend just went by too fast. I hadn't realized how homesick I was."

Her parents glanced at each other. Though they didn't say anything, Amy knew she hadn't fooled them. But she hadn't lied to them, either. She and Matt had talked about her staying in Ohio. Still, it had never occurred to her that he would actually leave without her.

And without Matt in her life, there didn't seem to be any reason to rush back to Lexington.

Monday faded into Tuesday and then Wednesday and Thursday. With each day that passed, Amy lost a little more hope that she'd hear from Matt. And what really surprised her was that Lila didn't call. But just in case she might be needed, she kept her cell phone charged and with her at all times.

Though she struggled with whether to stay in Ohio or go back to Lexington, she was determined to make good use of her time while home. She visited with her grandmothers and old friends, and in the privacy of her room she perused the local college's fall calendar and the employment ads in the newspaper.

It was on her morning prayer walk that she told her mother she was going back to school in the fall.

"That's great," Luanne said. "Have you decided what you're going to study?"

"I've narrowed it down to a couple of choices, but I won't have to declare a major immediately."

"I'm glad you're going back. I was always afraid you'd regret not going immediately after high school."

"I think now's the right time," Amy said.

"Your father and I will support you any way we can. We offered to pay for your education then, and we'll stand by that offer."

"Thanks," Amy said. It would be really easy to take their money. And while there was nothing wrong with their helping her financially, she knew it wasn't right for her. "I want to do this on my own."

"You're sure?" Luanne asked.

"Positive."

After a few steps in silence, Luanne said, "I don't know what happened in Lexington, but I like the changes."

"I grew up, Mom," Amy said. "I feel like I'm finding my place in the world, my place with God."

Luanne shook her head. "You're not my little girl anymore. I'm so proud of you."

Amy smiled, and the pain in her heart receded.

Now she knew why she'd had to come home. Only here could she meet the shadow of her old self and see how much she'd changed and grown in the last few months. She was a long way from being the woman of faith she desired to be, but with every prayer walk she moved a step closer.

Matt picked up the telephone a dozen times a day to call Amy and then slammed it down. Every time he walked through the stables, Leap of Faith neighed and her ears perked up as if to demand he bring Amy home.

Even his family had silently turned on him. When they didn't think he was looking, they stared at him as if they believed he was a fool. He'd had to practically forbid Aunt Lila from calling Amy, because he knew if his aunt called, Amy would come running back to Lexington.

This was for Amy's own good, he told himself at least a hundred times a day.

As it had for the last week, Amy's car sat in the driveway in the shade of the weeping willow tree. He'd promised her he'd return her things to her as soon as possible. But he just couldn't make the arrangements.

In the darkest hour of the night, he admitted what he was too proud to tell his family. He was hoping Amy would come back to collect what belonged to her.

Night after night, he and Leap of Faith waited, but she never came.

Amy and her mother fell into the habit of walking in the mornings. The more miles they covered together, the closer they grew. Finally, one week after Matt had left, she told her mother the truth.

"Matt left me on purpose," Amy said.

"I know," Luanne admitted. "But it's not the same as it was with Garry. Garry left you because he didn't love you. Matt left because he loved you too much."

Amy opened her mouth to refute her mother's opinion, but words deserted her. And before she could collect herself, her cellular telephone rang.

"Amy, it's me. Lila."

Amy immediately knew Lila's cheery greeting was

forced. Something was wrong. Amy's eyes fled to her mother for silent support.

"Are you okay?"

"I'm fine. Just a little tired. I've been poked and prodded until I can't stand it."

"What's going on? Where are you?"

"Now, there's nothing to worry about. I'm in the hospital, but they're releasing me today. The way everyone is hovering around me, you'd think I was an invalid."

Amy felt a smidgen of relief when she heard Lila's spirited complaint. "What happened?"

"The house has been in an uproar. Cara's four bridesmaids arrived a few days ago, and with the wedding and reception being held here on the farm, things have been hectic. I just thought I was overtired, but when I passed out—"

"Oh, my," Amy interrupted.

"It turns out I needed a pacemaker. I'm good as new, I promise."

Amy placed her hand over her heart and exhaled loudly. "You're telling me everything?"

"Absolutely. The thing is, though, Cara's a basket of nerves, and she needs help. And I can't give it to her. Could you come back for the week? I know it's asking a lot. But you did such a great job saving both Susy and Tam's weddings."

Amy didn't hesitate. "Of course, I'll be there."

But what she hadn't expected was her parents' response. "We're going with you," her father insisted.

"You're upset and worried, and we don't want you making the drive alone."

"I hate for you to miss work."

"I've got plenty of vacation days. Besides, we want to see this Kentucky horse farm that's captured your heart," her father assured her.

"Okay," Amy finally said. But her father was wrong about one thing. It wasn't the farm that had captured her heart as much as the man.

Lila hadn't exaggerated. By the time Amy and her parents arrived, Cara was frantic and near hysterics. Her dress didn't fit. Thunderstorms had been forecast for the entire weekend. The florist couldn't get the special orchids Cara had her heart set on, and the photographer's studio had been broken into and all his equipment had been stolen or vandalized.

Amy took one look at Cara's teary face and said, "Not to worry. Everything is going to work out fine. Trust me."

Trust me.

Matt had said those very words as he'd held her in the convenience store. But she couldn't think of that now. She had a wedding to save.

Amy took charge, sending the bridesmaids and her father on errands while her mother called every photographer in the yellow pages until she found one who'd just had a last minute cancelation.

"It looks like everything is under control," Amy said to her mother, Aunt Lila and Cara, who were sitting around the kitchen table.

Matt knocked lightly before entering the room. "I wish that were so."

All four women looked up with surprise. Cara instantly put her head on the table, clasping her hands behind her neck. In a tentative voice she said, "Unless you have good news, I don't want to hear it."

With the wedding only two days away, workmen had already assembled enormous white tents on the manicured lawn. Earlier in the morning, round tables and wooden folding chairs had been delivered for the reception and ceremony. The caterers and florists made last-minute location checks.

"What's wrong?" Amy asked without meeting Matt's gaze directly.

Though she'd been at Lila's for several days, she'd been extremely successful in avoiding him. It hadn't been easy, and at times it had been inconvenient. Only yesterday evening when she'd gone to the stables to see Leap of Faith, she'd had to slip into an empty stall to avoid bumping into Matt. If she'd known he was going to spend the next hour working in the center aisle, she wouldn't have hidden. But once she'd ducked into the stall she'd been stuck.

The wait had been torture, as her feelings had vacillated between anger and sadness. Even though he'd abandoned her, she couldn't help but miss his smile and the way his arms had once held her.

Shaking the unwelcome thoughts from her head, Amy placed both her hands on Cara's shoulders and said, "Whatever it is, we'll take care of it. Just like we've taken care of everything else."

Matt took a deep breath, and Amy knew this was no small obstacle.

"So, what's today's problem?" Amy forced an optimistic tone.

Matt handed her an invitation. "I don't know how anyone could have missed this. Maybe mine's just a printing fluke, or maybe they're all like this."

Amy quickly glanced at the engraved invitation that had been mailed six weeks ago. "I don't see anything wrong."

"The date. Check the date."

"August..." She placed her hand over her mouth. This couldn't be. This was a terrible mistake.

Cara's head popped up. "What? What is it?" She grabbed the invitation from Amy's hand. "Oh, my gosh," she exclaimed. "The date is wrong. According to this, the wedding is tomorrow afternoon and not Saturday." Though Cara babbled on, no one could understand a single word she said.

"The way I see it, we have two choices," Amy explained, as Cara looked at her with hopeful eyes. "Number one, we call everyone on the list and confirm the wedding's on Saturday." Like Amy, no one believed they could possibly reach over two hundred expected guests in time. "Then I think we have to have the wedding on Friday afternoon." Cara groaned, then left the room. "It's going to be fine," Amy called after her. "At least the forecast for Friday is sunny."

"It will be fine," Luanne said, "because it has to be."

Matt shrugged, as if to say he was only the messenger.

Cara and her bridesmaids were asleep when Amy slipped outside for a breath of fresh air. In the distance, the clock tower chimed the midnight hour, and the clouds parted to display a bright moon and swirling stars worthy of an artist. Inhaling the warm August air, Amy relaxed.

She couldn't put the decision off any longer. She had to decide if she would be staying in Lexington or going back to Ohio with her parents on Sunday.

Dear Lord, she silently prayed, *help me to see my choices clearly.*

When she opened her eyes, she saw Matt sitting in a rocking chair watching her. Placing a hand over her heart, she said, "How long have you been there?"

"Longer than you," he said, making no apology for not speaking sooner.

Refusing to let anything petty sidetrack her, Amy said, "There is something I'd like to say to you."

"If it's about the way I left you—"

Amy cut him off. "I know you thought you were doing what was best. You didn't do it to hurt me. But you don't know my heart." He didn't know how deeply she'd come to love him. "It's not up to you to decide where I live. And if I make the wrong choice, then I have to live with it. You can't prevent me from making mistakes."

Matt nodded. "It won't happen again."

"No, it won't, because I'm leaving the farm on Sunday."

She could tell he wanted to ask what her plans were, but his pride silenced him.

"I don't want to leave without thanking you. You've challenged me to examine my life. No longer am I going to float through life just letting it happen to me. From now on, I'm taking charge. And I can never express how much the time here on the farm with Aunt Lila has meant to me. It's one of the greatest gifts of my life. But I don't belong on this farm. This is your family, and when my family didn't suit me, I tried to trade them in for yours. Still, God has blessed my time here, and I'm glad for the months we've shared."

Before Matt could respond, Amy slipped into the house. Locking the door behind her, she pressed her back against the wall, letting her tears fall. In that painful moment, she made her decision. She would go home to Ohio. She couldn't stay in Lexington, because here she would be haunted by a love she could never have.

After Amy finished packing her things on Friday morning, she told her parents she'd be going home to Ohio. But she decided it would be best not to tell Matt or Aunt Lila until after the wedding. She didn't want to spoil Cara's wedding day. Or so she told herself.

With her father's help, Amy managed to carry her suitcases to her car without being noticed. With the wedding less than two hours away, the Wynn farm buzzed with activity. In a nearby tent, the string ensemble that would play during the ceremony and reception were setting up and tuning. Men and women in white uniforms carried container after container of hot hors d'oeuvres, cold salads and flavorful entrees to the reception tent, while waiters and waitresses in black tuxes finished setting the round tables with white linens and crystal. And right behind them came the florists with centerpieces made of fresh cut flowers selected to complement the bride's orchid bouquet.

Amy stowed the last suitcase in the car and told her father she'd be in the house in a few minutes to change for the wedding.

"Everything seems to be running smoothly, and at this point, I don't think anything else can go wrong. But if Lila or Cara does need me, tell them I've got my cell phone with me."

"Don't linger too long," he warned as he kissed her on the cheek and gave her a quick hug. "You've done such a great job saving this wedding from disaster, I'd hate for you to miss it."

Though Amy had no plans of intentionally skipping this wedding, it certainly wouldn't bother her to miss yet one more couple promising eternal love when her heart was breaking into a million pieces.

"I promise not to lose track of time." She smiled at her father, then said, "Did I tell you how glad I am that you're here?"

"You're just saying that because for the last two

days you've nearly worked me to death.'' Though he laughed, she knew he'd enjoyed helping. "You know, you're pretty good at this wedding stuff. You ought to consider going into the business.''

Amy laughed, and though she immediately tried to dismiss the idea, it stayed with her. Keeping a brisk pace, she made it to the top of Matt's hilltop in record time. She couldn't leave Lexington without one last visit.

As it had the first time, the lush view took her breath away. So much had changed since she'd first followed Matt up the winding path to this secluded piece of heaven. And most of the changes had been in her heart. She no longer had to look to the sky to find God, because she'd allowed Him back into her heart. Neither did the future look bleak. She was going back to Ohio and was excited about starting classes in the fall. Though she hadn't told anyone, she'd pretty much settled on taking a combination of business and horticulture classes. One day she might even manage or own her own retail nursery.

Then her father's words came back to her. *You're good at this wedding business.* And Matt had claimed that sometimes the answers she was looking for were staring her in the face.

In that instant, she knew exactly what she was going to do, and because she couldn't believe God had such a sense of humor she laughed out loud.

She was still laughing when she inhaled Matt's presence. The woodsy scent would always belong to him.

"Can anyone get in on the joke?" he asked. He stopped a few feet away from her and leaned against a tall boulder.

Amy wiped the tears and smile from her face. "I just decided what I'm going to do with my life. I'm going to become a wedding coordinator."

Matt rubbed the back of his head with his hand and laughed. "I've always heard God works in mysterious ways."

"Well, I wish He'd been a little more straightforward with me. I wasted a whole summer—"

Suddenly aware of how that sounded, she stopped mid-sentence.

"It's okay," Matt assured her. "I know what you meant. There's a few things I wish I'd figured out earlier, too."

She waited for him to explain and then was disappointed when he changed the subject.

"I saw you putting suitcases in the car. I take it you're leaving today." She nodded. "Were you going to leave without saying goodbye?"

She knew this wasn't the time to remind him that he'd left her in Ohio without saying goodbye. "Of course not. I thought I'd wait until after the wedding. I'm going back to Ohio. You were right, I belong with my family."

He nodded.

For all they'd been through, she hated for them to end with this awkward silence wedged between them.

"Maybe we should say goodbye now. It's going to

be a crazy afternoon, and we might not get another quiet moment.''

When words failed them, they relied on the language they'd trusted in the convenience storeroom. It felt right that they should end in the way they'd started—in each other's arms.

As Matt's arms tightened around her, Amy felt a spark of hope. He held her with all the love and tenderness a husband would express. Matt wasn't going to let her go.

And then he gently pushed her away and kissed her on the cheek. Too stunned to speak, Amy stared at him with her mouth wide open.

When her cellular telephone began to ring, she ignored it. Finally, Matt pulled it from her pocket.

''We're on our way. Try to stay calm. This'll all work out,'' he said.

Handing the phone back to Amy, he said, ''Cara and Paul have eloped.''

''You're kidding.''

Matt shook his head. ''The family's coming unglued. Everything is ready, and the guests will be arriving in a little more than an hour.''

''I can't believe they eloped,'' Amy said, still in shock.

''I hope you have some ideas on how to salvage this afternoon,'' Matt said.

''Me?''

''You're the one who just said you wanted to be a wedding planner.''

Amy bit her lip and walked to the edge of the high

ridge. Looking over the peaceful valley, she fought the idea. *It's crazy,* she told herself. *Absolutely crazy.*

But when she turned to Matt, she knew she had to take the chance. If she didn't, she'd regret this moment for the rest of her life.

"There can still be a wedding today," she said.

"You don't understand. Cara and Paul left for Napa Valley over an hour ago. They're going to get married in California."

"I'm not talking about Cara and Paul. I'm talking about you and me. I love you, Matt. Will you marry me, today?"

For what seemed like forever Matt stared at her. And when he took a step backward, Amy had her answer.

He didn't love her.

Had the intense connection she'd felt between them been all one-sided? Was it possible she'd imagined or misread their closeness this summer?

Amy waited just a few more seconds, and when Matt still said nothing, she turned and ran. Though she raced her tears down the hillside, her heart lagged behind.

It wasn't until Amy disappeared from sight that Matt snapped out of his daze and acknowledged the stabbing pain in his chest. She was the one.

Why couldn't he have realized it sooner?

A life without her flashed before his eyes. It would be a soundless, colorless life filled with regret and loneliness.

Her words echoed in his heart. "When you fall in love with the right one, she'll melt your fears."

She'd been right, because he had no doubt he was going to love her for a lifetime.

"Amy," he yelled. "Amy…wait for me."

He ran as fast as he could. He had to reach her before she fled the farm and he never saw her again.

"Amy," he called from the bottom of the hill. As they crossed the meadow, he gained on her. By the time she reached the edge of the herb garden, he was at her side.

Wrapping both arms around her, he finally stopped her. "I've got you now, and I'm never letting you go."

Though Amy's cheek remained pressed against his shoulder, he felt her embrace tighten. Kissing her on the top of the head, he raised her chin with his fingers so he could look into her brown eyes.

"I love you, Amy Jenkins. You're the one I've been looking for all my life."

Amy smiled. "So now that you have me, what are you going to do?"

That was the easiest question he'd ever had to answer. Lowering his mouth, he kissed his bride-to-be.

"Amy…Matt… Where have you been?" Aunt Lila rushed toward them. Close behind, Amy's and Matt's parents followed, along with a half dozen other family members.

Matt shared a conspiratorial grin with Amy before saying to Aunt Lila, "We've put our heads together, and we've come up with a plan to save the day.

Though we're going to need a little help and patience from you and the rest of the family.''

''And what exactly do you have in mind?''

But before he could tell her, Aunt Lila threw her arms around them and said, ''This is the best news I've heard all day. I knew the moment I met you, Amy, that you were the one for my Matt.''

Standing at her father's side, Amy waited impatiently as the flower girl and ring bearer made their way down the white carpet to the flower arbor. She didn't want to wait another second to become Matt's wife.

Her father patted her hand and said, ''Are you ready?''

She nodded.

The last two hours had flown by. She and Matt had rushed to the courthouse to obtain a marriage license. At Aunt Lila's suggestion, they'd tried on Cara's gown and Paul's tux, and by a miracle they'd been a perfect fit.

Inhaling deeply, she tried to calm her racing heart. Moving to the beat of the music, she took the first step of the rest of her marriage.

The ceremony flowed beautifully, from the melodic string ensemble to the sweet scent of fresh cut flowers to Matt's loving smile. And when the minister said, ''I now pronounce you husband and wife,'' Amy knew she would treasure this moment forever.

Matt kissed her, and then they turned to celebrate with their family, who mobbed them with hugs and tears before they could make the traditional walk down the carpet.

Though they couldn't imagine the day getting any better, Aunt Lila had one more surprise for them. Hitting a water glass with a knife, she gathered the attention of the large reception crowd.

"Because of the way this happy occasion came to be, there wasn't time to select wedding presents for Matt and Amy."

"I've got the best present in the whole world," Amy said, then kissed Matt on the lips. The family cheered, and Aunt Lila had to hit the knife against her glass to regain their attention.

"While that may be, there is something we all want you to have. What you don't know is that while you were at the courthouse, we held a family meeting. Although I own this farm, I would never sell or transfer the title without discussing it with my siblings, who grew up here with me."

When Amy placed her hand over Matt's chest it was beating so hard she thought it would explode.

Taking Matt's and Amy's hands, Lila said, "I want you to have this farm as my wedding gift to you."

Tears sprung from Matt's eyes, and he barely choked out his words. "I can't accept this land as a gift. I've always told you I would buy it."

Aunt Lila looked to the family for support and said, "Don't you think he would have learned by now not to argue with me?" Everyone laughed as Aunt Lila hugged the newlywed couple.

"Then you have to promise to live with us. This will always be your home," Amy said.

Lila shook her head. "Just as this is a new season for you, it's a new beginning for me, too."

"Well, what do you think?" Matt asked Amy.

"I think this is the perfect place to raise our family."

Amy smiled as her thoughts returned once again to the hour they'd spent in the closet. Even then, God had known she and Matt were a perfect fit, and now she knew it, too.

* * * * *

Dear Reader,

I hope you loved Matt and Amy's story as much as I enjoyed writing it. Though I've never lived in Lexington, I passed through Kentucky nearly every summer of my childhood with my parents as we drove from our upstate New York home to visit my grandparents in Arkansas. Even then, Lexington fascinated me with its rich history, lush bluegrass pastures and beautiful horse farms.

Most recently, I spent a week in Lexington with my mother-in-law, Florence Stovall, where we visited many of the same places Amy, Matt and Lila do in *A Groom Worth Waiting For*. We started our trip with a driving tour, which included many horse farms, historic churches and cemeteries, and ended in the downtown area where we visited homes built in the early 1800s, including the girlhood home of Mary Todd Lincoln. We ended our trip with ride up the Kentucky River on the *Dixie Belle* and a leisurely stroll through the Shaker Village at Pleasant Hill. And, of course, we enjoyed the local cuisine—hot brown sandwiches, beaten biscuits and, my favorite, chocolate pecan pie.

Thanks for joining Amy, Matt and me on this trip to Lexington!

Crystal Stovall

Next Month
From Steeple Hill's

Love Inspired®

A FAMILY ALL HER OWN
by *Bonnie K. Winn*

Minister Katherine Blake's life changes forever
when she falls head over heels for disillusioned
single dad Michael Carlson, who is struggling to do
right by his motherless daughter. Can Katherine
restore Michael's lost faith—and realize a cherished
dream in the process?

Don't miss
A FAMILY ALL HER OWN
On sale December 2001

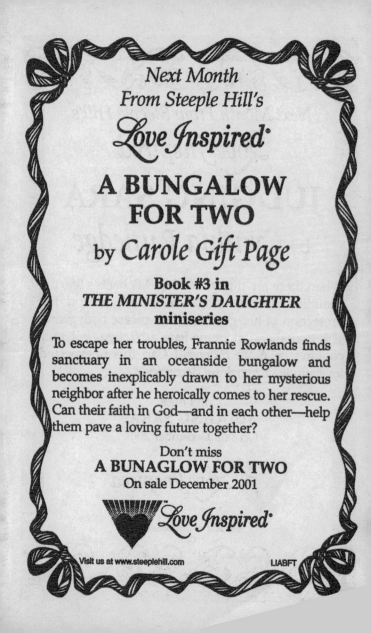

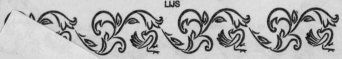